The Fetcher
Fletcher Barnes

Other Books By Tim Northburg

The Decnalab Codex

Zebulon Quest

Otterocity!

Otterocity! Field Guide

Fuel The Furnace

Decide On It!

Realize It!

The Fetcher
Fletcher Barnes

Written By
Tim Northburg

Illustrated By
Cael Johnson

Cover design by Cael Johnson
Illustrated by Cael Johnson

Published by Tim Northburg and Galification Media

www.TimNorthburg.com

www.GalificationMedia.com

Summary: A young slave, forced to search for unknown artifacts, discovers one that leads him on a journey with a shape-shifting wolf. Together, they must recover the remaining artifacts to free his people from slavery and overthrow those in power.

ISBN: 979-8-9882872-0-9

Library of Congress Number: 1-12445083591

This book is set in 12-point Garamond

CONTENTS

VI

DEDICATION

For all the boys and girls who need a little belief, strength, courage, and resolve. You can have it!

VIII

PROLOGUE

"It was once said you could be anything you want to be in life. You could be a butcher, a baker, or a candlestick maker. You could make your own destiny. However, in our world, in this age, your destiny is chosen for you—I am, and always will be, a Fetcher!"

NIGHT EYES

I looked forward to this time of night when the sun sets below the ocean and the moon rises over the hilltops. This night was slightly different though. I sat at my window with my head in my arms and looked out over San Fargo. The moon was full and sprinkled the valley with its glory, majestically illuminating the terracotta rooftops of San Fargo like plates of bronze. Suddenly, the temperature dropped, and a cool mist drifted down the river, covering the meadow in a thin blanket. Then, on cue, it showed itself.

I saw the subtle movement at the edge of the forest; a jagged silhouette sneaking through the huckleberry then pausing at the edge of the meadow. After a moment, the animal sniffed the air, and made its way along the edge of the trees. I watched the beast's hulky movements, as it zigzagged around the trunks. I wondered what freedom would be like. I yearned to move freely outside the city wall and follow my own destiny—like a wolf in the night.

The lone wolf drew me nightly to my perch at the window. It came from the heart of the forest—in a ceremony of two beings: one of freedom and one of servitude.

Lifting my chin off my folded arms, I leaned forward on the sill and steadied myself so as not to fall onto the cobblestone three floors below. I strained through the darkness to watch its movement, even though I knew where it was going. Its muscular gray body, silver streaked, moved towards me through the wild grass in this nightly ritual.

Searching the blanket of fog, I saw the large figure break through the edge of the dense undergrowth, the upper half of its body floating across the mystic whiteness. I noticed the fog splitting around the creature, billowing around its rapid feet, then settling back into dormancy, hiding the buffalo grass from view.

Wolf's tail jutted out from behind its strong haunches and wagged back and forth with a purpose. The tip looked as if someone dunked it into a vial of ink. There were prominent black markings on its body along with a diamond shaped patch on its forehead.

I saw the yellow orbs that were its eyes coming to me in the night. I watched Wolf move to the center of the meadow, then stop and sat amongst the silver tendrils of fog. It stares at me. Its dead eyes picked up the moonlight and reflected it across the meadow like two spotlights in the night.

This creature intrigued me. I long to escape the prison of the surrounding walls and be one with it, roaming the forest, hills, and glades, free from civilization and human influence. However, a part of me was scared; I was afraid of its wild, untamed manners. Or maybe I was just scared of being alone—scared of the unknown.

We locked gazes and I sat there for hours. I was communicating with unspoken words as it shared its strength and vulnerability, its wisdom and cunning, and its beauty and power with only a stare. I understood the heart of Wolf yet hungered to know for myself what it meant to be free.

As my eyelids began to feel like fishing weights, I laid my arms once again on the window ledge, rested my chin on my forearms, and watched it until I fell asleep.

Wolf's howl filled my ears and penetrated my soul.

It called my name—

Fletcher Barnes.

THE PLEDGE

I lifted my head off my forearms, wiped the drool from the side of my cheek and looked across the rooftops. My gaze drifted over the sandstone wall, past the rushing river that circles the small village, to the spot where my nightly visitor had been sitting. My friend was gone, only the patch of crumpled grass remained. My heart sank. I had hoped today would be different and Wolf would be there waiting for me.

"Fletcher!" a voice called from the cobblestone street below.

Hearing my name, I peered over the windowsill. Standing at the base of the stone tower, I saw a boy, maybe half my age—about seven or eight—staring back at me.

"What?"

"You forgot to ring the bell," he shouted through cupped hands. "Breakfast is starting!"

"Darn—thanks!"

Springing up, I hit the back of my head on the window. I did a little dance in the middle of my attic room and rubbed the pain away. Head throbbing, I rushed up the small wooden ladder in the far corner, threw open the trap door and disappeared through the small opening into the bell tower. I yanked the rope as hard as I could to bring the brass instrument to life.

With the morning bell still sounding in the streets of San Fargo, I raced down the ladder and changed into my clothes. I quickly pulled my khaki shorts on over my briefs, threw on my dingy gray t-shirt with the ruby F painted on the front and back, and thrust my feet into woven hemp sandals. As I headed for the door, I stopped briefly at the mirror, licked the palms of my hands, and smoothed down my hair sticking up in the back.

I hurried down the small stairwell leading out onto the cobblestone road and flew down the hill to the great hall. I cut into line behind Marcus Dunn—my lifelong Idol.

Marcus Dunn was the oldest Fetcher here at San Fargo, and the first of our kind. Marcus turned and looked at me. His gentle, hazel eyes met mine, and he smiled through a salt-and-pepper beard that matched his jet-black hair that was turning gray at the temples.

"Running late?"

"Yeah," I said, catching my breath. "I overslept."

"That's not like you."

"I know," I said, shuffling forward with him in the breakfast line. "I've never sleep in."

"Maybe this is a sign."

"What do you mean?"

"Well, maybe You're nervous about your first dive."

"I am—a bit."

"Maybe because you slept in, this could be the day," he paused, and a more serious look washed over him. "Maybe you will be the one to find *it* today."

"Maybe it means nothing. Maybe, I was up late watching the stars and just overslept."

"Maybe," Marcus said, and grabbed a tray off the

counter. "Sometimes things are coincidence, other times they are meant to happen."

Maybe things happen for a reason—but not to me. I stepped forward with my tray, took my solitary scoop of porridge, scrawny pancake, and two strips of bacon, and proceeded to the table where Marcus was already digging into his food.

"Do you think we will ever find it?" I asked, staring at the colorless blob of pasty oats.

"Someone will—eventually."

"Yeah," I agreed. "Do you think it will be one of us?" I looked around at the sea of shirts with an F painted on them, wondering who it would be.

"Maybe," Marcus took a drink of water to help his food down. "And when we do, maybe we will be free, like the wolves." Marcus winked at me and took another bite.

The rest of breakfast, I sat there in silence gnawing on my leathery pancake—chewing on what he had said. I pondered the thought of being free. I thought about what it would be like to travel through the land, roam the forests, and climb the tallest mountain. I wondered if it could really happen. Then I thought about Wolf. How did Marcus know about Wolf?

The High Commander strutted to the front of the hall and stepped up onto the podium. He stood staring with authority down the depths of the hall, his gaze intense under his tan flat-brimmed hat.

"My fetchers . . . I have an announcement to make," he addressed us with his booming military voice. "As you already know, tonight is the Guifachs Festival. This annual festival commemorates the 52nd anniversary of Lorucias Guifachs who, upon burning down his library in Gullet, found the tablet of Goah, setting us on our quest to find the four relics of antiquity hidden in the four corners of our land. However, tonight marks a special occasion. Every fourth year, we are proud to host the Prime Ministerial in our corner of the land."

Many in the crowd cheered. However, I noticed that it barely masked those who jeered in response to the commander.

"All right," the High Commander said, holding out his hands, suppressing the outburst. "It is expected of you to report to the hall following your duties. We will have dinner, proceeded by a short ceremony, and the Prime Ministerial will give his speech. It is *expected*—I repeat—it is *expected* that you all be on your best behavior tonight—Call to Order!"

Everyone in the room stood at full attention, holding their right fist out in front of them, as if flexing their biceps. Those who had shoes clicked their heels together before the room fell silent.

"Fetchers, promise and swear before the Ministerial that you will today, and for the rest of your life, abide by the Fetcher's Creed."

"I will," I replied in unison with my fellow fetchers.

"Now, for our solemn pledge."

Everyone took a deep breath and looked at the large inscription painted onto the white wall behind the podium and regurgitated the Fetcher's Creed.

"I believe in the Ministerial and its standards, fundamentals, and values. I believe in the brotherhood of Fetchers, as it is our duty to carry out the traditions of Fetchers before me. I take my orders from the Ministerial and uphold my post with belief, strength, courage, and resolve. I know it is my job to find and present the relics of antiquity, to the Ministerial, ensuring its authority for all of time."

"Fetchers, you are here to uphold your destiny—

seek and ye shall find."

"*Seek and ye shall find!*" we shouted and pounded our chests with our fists.

"Dismissed!"

As the other Fetchers filed out of the great hall, Marcus placed a hand on my shoulder and whispered into my ear.

"You know, where the Prime Ministerial goes, so goes the Oraculum!"

"Right," I said, and thought back to the last festival with the Prime Ministerial.

I remembered seeing the strange twins and had caught them staring at me on many occasions. A shiver ran down my spine—they creeped me out.

"Be careful . . . don't get too close to the Oraculum."

I watched Marcus walk away with the other Fetchers wondering what he meant.

What does he know? I asked.

THE LEGEND OF GOAH

San Fargo was built on a hill at the end of a valley where two rivers converged and circled the city like a handcuff. A great limestone wall encompassed the entire city. It served two purposes: keep the river water out, and keep the fetchers and everyone else in. It was easier for the Ministerial Guard to walk around the entire city and patrol the area from their elevated vantage point atop the walls. However, during the ten years I lived here, only one person tried to escape.

A few years ago, another Fetcher breached the wall and tried to swim across the river, but the current was too strong, and it swept him out to sea. Several guards found his body later. The waves had dashed him against the jagged rocks along the cliffs at the edge of the sea. He wasn't the only one. There had been several boys before him that had tried to swim across the river and drowned. At least that's what they told us.

I followed Marcus and the other Fetchers down the cobblestone road that ran along the city wall until we came to a halt at the city's only gate. I stood near Marcus and waited as the Ministerial Guard lowered the massive oak drawbridge.

Several guards led the way. The rest brought up the rear, ensuring there was no way for us to escape. We trudged across the drawbridge to follow the narrow dirt road cut into the side of the steep hill. We marched as a group for several minutes until the road narrowed at the mouth of the cliffs.

As we came out of the mouth of the steep ravine, the waves crashed and sprayed us with sea foam and saltwater mist every thirty seconds. After some distance, we came to a small wharf, on a half-moon strip of beach surrounded by cliffs. Opening to the sea, it provided a flat area for the outbuildings and docks that anchored the twenty-five boats.

The equipment specialists immediately handed out the proper gear to the Fetchers. I remembered the seven years I had spent lugging the heavy diving equipment and was glad when I turned thirteen and I didn't have to do the grunt work anymore. Although, I didn't realize that diving for artifacts, these last two years, searching through rubbish at the bottom of the ocean was going to be any better work.

In preparation for our day's labor, we stripped down to our skivvies in the middle of the granite dock. We donned rubber suits, slipped on weight boots, pulled on our gloves, and grabbed our underwater gear. When I was done, I took my diving-bell helmet from the young lad who was waiting patiently and struggled to keep my hold on it. I realized he was the same boy who had called up to me from the street earlier. Balancing the helmet in one arm, I reached out and ruffled his dark brown hair.

"Thanks for the wake-up call." I said and winked at the boy.

"I knew something wasn't right, dive-master Barnes," he said. "You never forget to ring the bell." He stared up at me with youthful admiration—the same look I wore for Marcus all those years I served him.

"Thanks, I appreciate it."

The boy smiled and went back to work. I turned and headed down the dock to the last boat, climbed in and sat down next to Marcus.

"Ready to do this?" I asked.

"Ready as my first day."

The boat rocked as a dockworker untied the rigging and pushed us away with his foot. It was a breezy day. The water was a bit rougher than usual. We had to keep hold of our helmets, so they wouldn't fly around the deck and crash into someone's leg, breaking it. I had seen that happen before, and it was not pretty.

"Tell me again of the legend of Goah and the stone tablet," I asked Marcus. I liked hearing the story on the boat ride out to our Fetching-ground, and Marcus always obliged.

"Goah is the ancient spirit of the winds," Marcus started. "From the beginning of time, and the earth was made, Goah was the higher power in charge. He controlled nature, the elements, and the cycle of Earth. Lore says he was a giant who lived in a grand hall in the Western Sky. The hall had four doors, one on each wall, and he used them to control the four corners of the Earth."

"When man came to the Earth, Goah sometimes brought good fortune upon him, and he sometimes brought bad fortune. Goah was respected by the people, nonetheless. Over time, man became developed special abilities, and even used magic. It is said, that thousands of years ago, one man, Hrogolath, studied dark magic and tapped into an unnatural force. He became very powerful—almost God-like. His power was so great that he found a way to live longer than any other human. His thirst for power caused him to search out Goah's great hall for more. Hrogolath wanted to control the earth and the heavens.”

“Why did he want to do that?” I asked.

“Sometimes, power and control twists men’s souls and makes them do things that they normally wouldn’t do.”

“What makes them do that?”

“Fear, my boy—fear,” Marcus said. “Fear replaces all emotions. If fear takes hold, you can’t have belief, strength, courage, or resolve.”

“What would they have to fear?”

“Maybe they are afraid of losing power and losing control. I believe that’s what happened to Hrogolath. He gained so much power, he was afraid of losing it. He became paranoid that someone would want his power too. He also knew that Goah was the only one that could take it away, and if he got rid of Goah, he himself would gain supreme power and ultimate control.”

“Hrogolath used his dark magic to make his way up to the Western Sky and entered the great hall. Goah was ready for Hrogolath and they went to war. However, Goah underestimated Hrogolath’s power; they fought for ten days, and ten nights locked in a battle of no sums.”

I sat there on the edge of my seat waiting for the ending. Even though I had heard this story a hundred times, I always looked forward to the ending.

“Both tired, they continued fighting into the eleventh day. Strangely, Goah started to weaken. When Hrogolath was about to finish him off, Goah concentrated his magic to conjure a great storm that blew into the four doors and trapped Hrogolath in the center of the hall.”

“Now, Goah realized that that was not going to hold Hrogolath forever, but he didn’t have enough strength to kill him. He was afraid that if his power was captured by Hrogolath, Hrogolath would tear apart the world, so he did the only thing he could think of. He took four artifacts and enchanted them with the power to control the four elements—water, earth, fire, and air. He called out to the wind, and four animals came to each of the four doors. A Moose stood at the western door, a Panther came to the north door, a Bear showed up at the southern door, and an Eagle landed at the eastern door."

"Goah gave the first artifact to Moose. He oversaw water and granted Moose control of the marshes and gray mists of the west. It was his duty to hide the artifact in the waters and to watch over it. The Western winds carried Moose to Earth."

"The second artifact, he gave to Panther. Because of his strength, Panther oversaw earth and gained control of the forests and hills. Goah instructed him to find a resting place in the North and hide the artifact deep within. And the Northern winds carried Panther to Earth."

"The third artifact went to Bear. He too was strong, but his super strength was born of fearlessness, so he oversaw fire. He told Bear to take the artifact to the South and hide it amongst the flames. The Southern winds carried Bear to Earth."

"Finally, Goah came to Eagle. Eagle already controlled the sky. He understood the summer winds, soared with the spring, and fall breeze, and flew on the winter gales. Thus, he oversaw Air. Goah told him to fly high and hide the artifact of air within the sky. The Eastern winds carried Eagle to Earth."

"This left Goah very weak, so much so that the storm that held Hrogolath was weakened too. It was a matter of time before Hrogolath freed himself. Drawing on his last bit of strength, Goah summoned a tornado that crashed through the Great Hall. Even as the tornado swept Hrogolath's body away, carrying him into the sun to burn forever, Goah knew that there was a chance that Hrogolath's evil spirit could come back. With that final thought, Goah's body fell out of the sky."

"But that wasn't the end of Goah. His spirit lived on . . . right?"

"Right," Marcus said, and smiled. He had a twinkle in his eye and his face looked as if he were somehow part of this story. "Where he fell, in the hidden forest, there grew a great tree that holds his spirit and his power. Its roots spread out to the four corners of the land. It is said that he is still influencing everything that goes on."

"Has anyone found the tree?"

"Not that I know of," Marcus said. "It is hidden to the naked eye until the time it is needed. But legend has it that the tree holds a great power. Some think it has the key to eternal life—and some people will do anything to get hold of that power."

"Thanks, that's a great story." I said, staring past him to the coastline and the forests that spread to the east.

"Some people say it is a story, or a legend—others believe it is truth and the tree is out there somewhere," whispered Marcus.

The steam engine chugged and strained as the captain guided us out to the open waters.

DEEP SEA DIVING

The boat smoothed out as we got further from the shore, and my stomach settled as the rocking eased. When we reached our spot, the captain dropped anchor. As Fetchers, it was our sole job to dig through the mud and the debris of an age long past. We swore to continually look for some artifact— no one knows what it looks like—and hand over the sea glass, silver, metal, and any other items that may be of value to the Ministerial. It was a cold, wet, and boring life.

"Stay calm down there," Marcus said, and nudged me in the shoulder.

"Easier said than done," I replied.

We put on our helmets, grabbed our baskets and underwater lamps, and shuffled to the end of the boat. The equipment specialists fired up the air generator and hooked us up. One-by-one the Fetchers in front of me jumped into the water. When it was my turn, I stepped forward. I felt the rush of cool air blow through my hair from the air compressor.

"Keep the air flowing!" I shouted through the glass window of my helmet.

"Yes, dive-master Barnes," The specialist smiled and gave me a thumbs up.

I jumped off the end of the outrigger and floated in

the cool water with the other Fetchers. The giant wheel at the back of the boat spun to life unrolling all twenty-five air hoses, dropping us down to the bottom of the sea.

In seconds, darkness consumed me. The only sounds I heard were my own breathing, the swishing of the air entering my helmet, and the popping of the bubbles escaping out of the vents. I felt like my head was going to explode from the pressure, or maybe it was from my nerves. For what seemed like an eternity, the weights pulled me down into the dark abyss until my feet touched the ground.

Several lights flickered around me as the other Fetchers fired up their lamps and began working. I clipped my basket to my belt and sat it down on the mud floor. The silt from our landing floated around our bodies, making it difficult to see. I turned on my lamp and began digging through the mud. As I churned through the mud, it became impossible to see more than a foot in front of me.

The previous week, our expedition team had found this old dumpsite, and it became our new search area. I sifted through the fine silt, reaching the clay undersurface. Scraping at the hardened mud, I dug down a foot or so in a square pattern and continued fingering my way through the thick muck. After half an hour of nothing, I hit pay dirt. I pulled a thin object from the silt and rubbed off the caked clay. It was a silver knife. I figured it would fetch at least fifty gillys from the Ministerial when I cashed in my day's find so I put it in my mesh basket and continued digging. Expanding my search, I dug a bit deeper, in an arching pattern. I hit something hard. Laying my lamp on the ocean floor, I scraped at the object with both hands.

"Ouch!" I said, reeling in pain.

I lifted my hand to my viewing window to inspect my finger. A small cut oozed blood into the seawater. I was glad that the gloves were separate from our suits, or I would have had a greater problem—depressurization. As I inspected the torn bit of glove and my index finger, I realized I would be all right. I tried to shake away the thought there might be sharks in these waters and continued digging around the object. Carefully, so as not to cut my hand again, I pulled out a rusted can out of the clay with its jagged top hanging by a shard of metal. Assessing its little value, I threw it into the basket with the knife and picked up my light.

Not wanting to disrupt any more silt, I moved slowly as I shone the light down into the hole. Finding two items in a single square foot was rare and I felt there was something more down there.

The light illuminated the sides of the hole and passed over a lump protruding at the bottom. Intrigued, I held the light on the object, and with my free hand, I scraped around the edges and freed it from its confinement in the clay. I hunched over to inspect it in the light cast by the lamp I lowered on to the ground.

The object fit in the palm of my hand and narrowed at the top. With my thumb and forefingers, I rubbed the light brown muck off its surface to reveal a small cobalt-blue bottle. I knew instantly it was rare. In all our finds, there was brown, green, and clear sea glass tumbled smooth by the waves. On occasion, we found jade and amber glass as well as soft blue fragments. However, cobalt-blue glass was the rarest glass of all. Turning it over I scraped at the backside and realized it was intact—another rare find.

The bottle touched the bare skin of my cut finger

when I turned it over again in my palm. I felt a tingling sensation rush up my arm, through my body.

I heard a voice inside my helmet. *You are the one . . . Fletcher Barnes.*

I looked around, but no one was there.

"What?" I said aloud into my helmet. "Who said that?"

No one answered. Thinking I must be losing my mind from oxygen deprivation or something, I put the bottle with my other finds and continued working, searching for more stuff.

Over the next several hours, I found other bits and pieces that I thought the Ministerial would like, but I couldn't forget the strange tingling sensation that overcame me when the bottle touched my skin, nor the voice I had heard in my helmet.

Who said it? I thought. *What did it mean by, You are the one . . .?*

THE ARTIFACT

I broke the surface, glad to be getting back on the boat. I climbed the ladder to the deck, hiding my loot behind my back. The instant the equipment specialist unplugged my air hose, I plopped the basket down and kicked it under the wooden bench. Marcus helped take my helmet off and we sat down, as the air hoses finished rolling up in their individual slots.

"Did you find anything good?" asked Marcus.

"Huh . . . what?" I said, coming out of my trance.

Marcus looked at me, "Are you all right, my boy?" he stared into my eyes. "You look as if you'd seen a ghost."

"Er . . . yeah. I cut my finger digging." I said, holding my finger up for him to see.

"It's only a scratch." Marcus took out a small hanky and dabbed my cut. "I've seen that look before, something else bothering you?"

"Yeah," I said, then reached underneath the bench and pulled the bottle from the mesh basket. "I found this." I held the bottle in both hands and subtly revealed the bottle so the other Fetchers wouldn't see.

"Oh my," Marcus said excitedly.

He grabbed my hands, pulling the object close so he could inspect it. Turning my back to the others, I opened my hands showing the cobalt face of the bottle. Looking down at it now, I noticed for the first time the raised, white marking. It was a tree with four large roots and multiple branches enclosed in a single wiggly line that denoted the leaves.

"When it touched my cut, I felt a tingling go through my body. Oh, and I heard a voice inside my helmet."

Marcus raised an eyebrow. I could tell he was trying hard to contain his excitement.

"What did the voice say?"

I leaned forward and told him softly, "You are the one . . . Fletcher Barnes."

"Oh my," Marcus breathed, and looked around to make sure the others were busy with their own finds.

He tilted my hand up, looking at the mouth of the bottle. A cork shadowed the inside of the stem, and there was a black, tarry substance that covered the top, sealing it tight.

"*Oh my!*" Marcus said, covering the bottle with his hand. "Do you know what this is?"

"No."

I saw the look of excitement on his face turn to panic as his eyes darted around the boat. "You have to hide this in your suit," he said, grabbing the bottle from me. "This is the artifact—you have to keep it a secret." He unzipped the top of my suit and stuffed it down my shirt.

I was in shock.

Marcus sat up straight to regain his composure and not draw any attention from the guard or the other Fetchers. Marcus didn't say anything for a minute, then turned back to me and whispered, "I knew this day would come."

"What?" I asked, not sure what he was talking about.

Marcus looked over my shoulder and leaned forward. "That bottle has the marking of the World Tree on it."

"The World Tree?"

Now I was certain that he had the bends or something. Either that or he was pulling a joke on me.

"Look at me," he said, realizing I thought he was crazy. "The World Tree is the marking of Goah. That is one of the four artifacts he released into the four corners of Danforth."

I shook my head, not believing what he was saying.

Marcus grabbed my shoulders, shook me, and whispered excitedly into my ear, "My boy, you found it. Now you mustn't let the Ministerial get their hands on it."

"How do you know this?" I asked him.

In my mind, all I had found was an ordinary bottle, thrown away and covered by the sea. How could this be the artifact?

Marcus looked at me, his expression serious. "Ever since I came to San Fargo, I've had strange dreams. Every night I saw this symbol in my dreams. At first, I didn't know what it meant. Then I started seeing other things. Lately, I saw images of you, and the boats. I saw the Oraculum and a blue bottle—just like this one."

"They were just dreams," I said dismissing his assumptions.

"No Fletcher. When I put the images together with the stories, my father told me, I knew it was you. You were going to find the artifact. That is why I choose you as my apprentice—so I could help you and be there on this day!"

"It can't be that."

"Listen, things have come true from my dreams

before. Now, you must listen to me. The Oraculum will be looking for this. You must hide it when you change, and keep it in your under shorts until you get back to your room—do you have a place to hide this?"

"Yes, I have a spot in the bell tower."

"Ok, we will think what to do, after the Prime Ministerial and the Oraculum leave in a day or so. Right now, we must act like nothing has happened—got it?"

I nodded, zipped up my suit, and sat in disbelief the whole ride back to the docks. All I thought about was the lump under my right arm as the cold glass chilled my skin.

If what Marcus said was true, and this was the artifact, we completed our job here. Then, if I gave the bottle to the Ministerial, we would be freed. Something in the seriousness of Marcus's voice urging me to hide the bottle made me uncertain. Part of me wanted to give the artifact to the Ministerial. However, remembering his story about Goah and the power of the tree, I made my mind up to keep it hidden—at least for now.

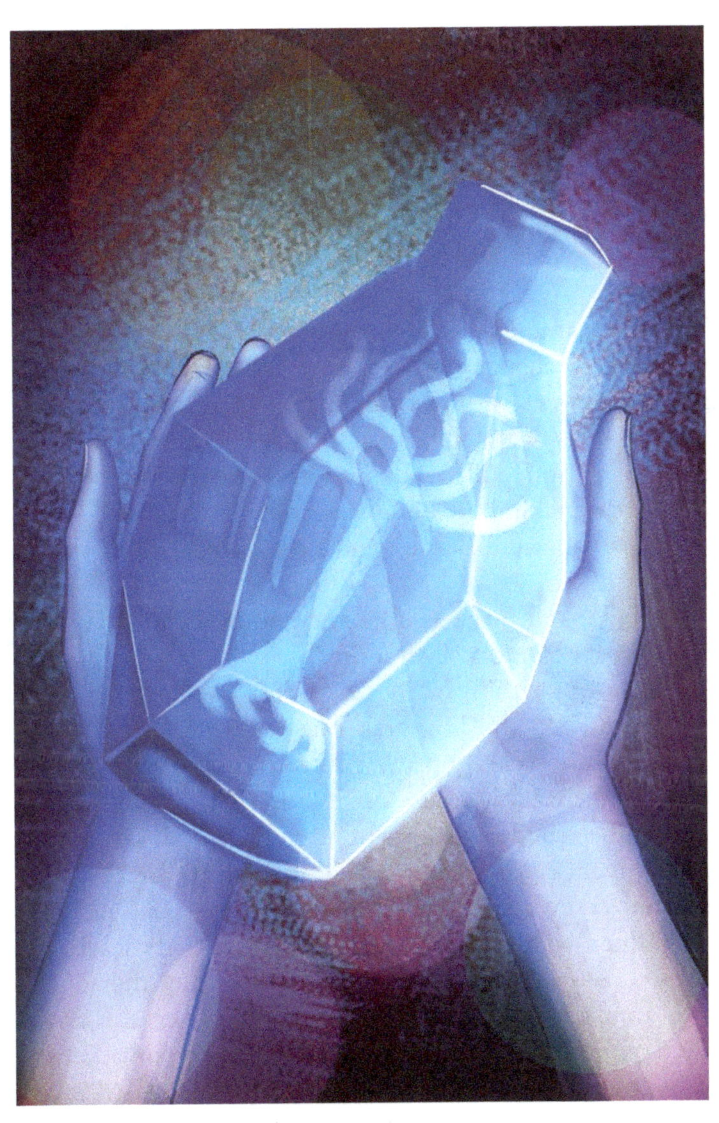

DISCOVERED

The boat came to rest against the jetty, and we filed onto the dock to change out of our gear. I carried my basket, less one object, to my equipment handler. Making sure nobody was watching, I slipped the bottle down my underwear and pulled on my khaki shorts. Luckily, the baggy material hid the bulkiness of my contraband.

"Dive-master Barnes, did you have a good dive?" the boy asked.

He looked at me as if he knew something was up.

"Yes, I found a silver knife."

"Wow, neato!"

I watched the boy grab our gear and lug it to the storeroom. I picked up my basket and carried it over to the guard shack. Marcus was by my side. I could tell he was still excited about my find however, I sensed his protectiveness over me like a warm breeze. He scrutinized everyone that came near.

When we reached the shack at the end of the dock, I realized something was not right. Normally there were two ministerial guards standing watch over the Stock Clerk who inventoried our objects and estimated the value of the objects found; and the Finance Clerk, who paid us our meager Fetcher's fee. The Prime Ministerial and his guards, as well as the Oraculum were there, watching the objects as the Fetchers laid them on the table. The Oraculum, with their matching baldheads, identical silver suits, matching purple ties, and flat, angular black shoes, stood at attention at the Prime Ministerial's side. With their shoulders touching and their heads tilted slightly towards each other, they looked like conjoined twins, and moved as one.

Their gaze sought and caught mine as they sucked me into a battle of stares. Locked in, my vision darted back and forth, from one pair of eyes, to the other. I tried my hardest to move, to turn my head, to do something, but their hold on me was unrelenting. I couldn't take my eyes off them it was as if they controlled me and wouldn't let go.

Looking at their faces, I realized for the first time that they had scars around each of their opposite eyes. Facing them, the one on the left had a scar on his left eye, and the one on the right had a similar pattern on his right eye. When their heads tilted further towards one another, their scars formed a diamond pattern.

When they touched their heads together, I was looking at each of their eyes inside the shape, and then— they were inside my head.

"We know you are the one . . ."

Suddenly, I felt a hand on my back.

"You need to move forward, m'boy," Marcus said nudging me. "You're holding up the line."

The sudden push broke the mental connection with the Oraculum. I turned and looked up at Marcus. He pursed his lips together and shook his head at me.

"What did I tell you?" he said softly. "Be careful, they are dangerous."

I turned around, stepped forward and kept my eyes latched on to the back of the Fetcher in front of me to keep myself from catching the Oraculum's gaze again. I wanted to tell Marcus, right there and then, what had just happened, but I couldn't. I was trapped and didn't know what to do. The object weighed down my shorts, and I was afraid that the glass would drop out and smash on the granite dock.

Finally, it was my turn. I stepped up to the table, plopped my basket onto the flat surface, and stared at the lady, so I wouldn't have to look at *them* again.

"Well, what do we have here?" the heavy lady asked.

I could feel everyone on the dock turn and look. The Prime Ministerial and his Guard leaned in to see. It was clear they were looking for something. Out of the corner of my eye, I noticed that the Oraculum didn't move an inch.

"Oh my, it is a silver knife," she said, then scribbled on the pad in front of her. She reached her hand into my basket and pulled out the tin can. "This. This is trash." She flung it down onto a discard pile on the ground and reached into the basket again, this time taking out a handful of sea glass. "Mmmm," She murmured, inspecting it. "Green, amber, green, brown, purple—that is unique—clear, and lime green." She noted the colors in her journal as she said them. She peered into the bottom of the basket. "That is all," she said, then passed the book to her partner.

The Finance Clerk looked over the other's notations then reached into the money tray. "That'll be five Gilly's for you." She handed me the coin and I left to go stand with the other waiting Fetchers while Marcus turned in his find.

I saw the Oraculum on the right tap the Stock Clerk on the shoulder then mumble something to her. Just as he stood straight again, the woman stood up from her chair and pointed at me.

"Guard, grab that boy and bring him back over here."

Two guards approached me. I thought about running, but where would I go? Then they grabbed my arms tightly so I couldn't escape. I didn't want to try to wiggle free in case the bottle fell out of my underpants. The guards pushed me forward until I stood at the side of the table in front of the Oraculum and the Prime Ministerial.

"Boy," the Prime Ministerial said, stepping forward to address me. "Are you carrying something?"

"No." I lied.

"Guards, search him," he sneered.

One of the guards frisked around my shirt then my shorts, feeling the lump between my legs. He rudely reached in and pulled out the cobalt bottle. I saw Marcus try to move around the table to protect me, but the guards surrounding the Prime Ministerial blocked his advance.

The guard inspected the bottle then handed it over. "Here you are, Prime Ministerial."

"Ah yes," he said waving off the guard.

The short, squatty Prime Ministerial hovered over the object he held in the palm of his hand and hovered over the object. He stroked the artifact affectionately with his fingers as his slicked-back gray hair flopped down onto his wrinkled brow. His beady black eyes bulged from their sockets as they roamed over every square inch of the bottle.

After a few minutes of silence, the Prime Ministerial stood up straight, cradled the artifact against his chest and stepped over to me.

"What is your name?"

"Er . . . Fletcher Barnes."

"Fletcher Barnes. You have found the first artifact. Your name will go down in history." He turned to his guards. "Lock him in his room until the ceremony."

The Prime Ministerial strode off to the city, the Oraculum and his Ministerial Guard in step behind him. The same two guards lifted me by the arms and whisked me away from the surrounding Fetchers.

THE LIGHT OF BELIEF

Fletcher was escorted through the Great Hall to the serving line. The roars and laughter suddenly died as the Fetchers saw me—all eyes directed my way. Their silent gazes locked in on my face felt odd, and I didn't know whether to run and hide, or strut through the crowd holding my head high with the last bit of my dignity. I decided on the latter, knowing that my time here was limited.

Mustering up my courage, I walked through the crowd to the serving line, grabbed my plate, chose a steak off the platter, and piled the mashed potatoes and green beans as high as they would let me.

Hey, I figured it was my last supper—might as well make it a good one.

I grabbed a knife and fork and made my way through the Fetchers to my table. As I passed the sea of gray shirts, with ruby Fs on them, the whispers started.

"He found the artifact!"

"He is the one!"

"Fletcher will set us free."

"Today is a great day!"

"Fletcher is our hero."

As I passed the last table and was about to sit down, a Fetcher behind me stood up. I felt him tower over me while he placed his beefy hand on my shoulder.

"Way to go, Fletcher Barnes!" he said, and slapped my back.

With that, the whole hall rose to their feet.

"*To the Fetcher, Fletcher Barnes!*" they cheered.

They all clapped, whooped, and knocked back their grog.

All my thoughts of dying washed away as I heard my name called throughout the great hall. My morbid visions of torture were replaced with an overwhelming sense of pride and accomplishment, and now, thoughts of freedom. I never thought that I would be the one to find the artifact. I didn't imagine I would be cheered by the entire San Fargo brotherhood of Fetchers.

At the height of it all, the High Commander slammed his gavel on the podium. "That's enough—back to your food!"

The mood in the room changed instantly as the cheers subsided and the Fetchers returned to their feast. I sat down next to Marcus and stared at my plate. Although everything looked scrumptious, I was too excited, too nervous, to eat.

"You are a hero, my boy," Marcus said, between bites of green beans.

"I don't know about that," I said, picking at my mashed taters and brown gravy.

We sat in silence for over twenty minutes, as we finished our meals. Then we cleared our trays from the table.

Waiting for the ceremony to begin, Marcus patted my back, "It's going to be alright, my friend."

I appreciated the attempt. Still, the knot in my gut tightened and I felt like I was going to toss my dinner all over the table.

The Ministerial Guard burst in and filed in from the antechamber. They formed a single line along the back wall. The lights dimmed and three robbed figures trailed in. Brown material hung down past their knees, and mysterious hoods hid their faces. The front of each robe was ornamented with a white box with a plus sign in the center, and purple silk adorned the edges of the sleeves and lined the insides of the hoods.

This was not the ceremony of Guifauchs Night that I had witnessed before.

As the figures sauntered across the raised stage, I realized that the two of similar height were the Oraculum and the last one—of stout nature—was the Prime Ministerial. The twins found their places near the corner. Standing side by side, they folded their hoods back simultaneously, revealing their newly shaved heads. From their vantage point on stage, they stared directly down the edge of the tables to where I sat.

Not wanting to make eye contact again, I turned my head to the center of the room where the Prime Ministerial stood in front of the podium and addressed the Great Hall from the depths of his hood.

"My trusted Oraculum . . . fellow members of the Ministerial Guard . . . and Brotherhood of Fetchers . . . we have been waiting for this monumental day for many a year, and now it is upon us. It started with my father's quest for the artifacts – Goah rest his soul – and was passed on to me to see it come to fruition. Now the day has come. Thanks to one of your kind, the first of four artifacts was found today, and that pleases me to no end. I must say that the Ministerial is one step closer to accomplishing its tasks, to develop the well-rounded operations of government, ensure the advancement of humanity, and provide the protection of our livelihood.

It is because of all your dedication and hard work that tonight has become a reality."

The Prime Ministerial nodded at the closest guard, "Now we will present the artifact."

Four guards slipped into the antechamber and returned a moment later. Two of them carried a smallish, black table, and placed it in front of the podium. Another guard unrolled a thin altar cloth and placed it on the black lacquered surface. Next, he dropped a purple cushion on the floor, straightened it with his foot, and returned to the other guards. The fourth guard stepped from the doorway carrying a lit silver lamp. He held it in front of his body, walked ceremoniously over to the table, set it on the cloth, and faded back in line behind the Prime Ministerial.

The Prime Ministerial stood up straight, stepped around the podium and stopped in front of the altar. "Normally we celebrate Guifachs Night as a yearly tradition, at each of the Fetchers camp in the four corners of this great nation of Danforth. Traditionally, we honor this night with the flame of this lamp to keep our purpose burning true. The flame, which burns constantly, represents the efforts we put forth in our search for the artifacts."

"Tonight, brings a different meaning." The Prime Ministerial pushed his hood back, stared down at the group of Fetchers, and finally fixed his gaze upon me. "Fetcher Fletcher Barnes, come forward."

With a lump in my throat, I stood and walked along the wall, keeping my eyes averted from the Oraculum. I could feel their gaze, but I didn't want to return it. I shuffled towards the table, and with my back turned to the other Fetchers, faced the Prime Ministerial.

"Please kneel," he ordered.

"Yes, Prime Ministerial," I replied, and followed his order.

Kneeling on the soft, purple cushion, I lowered my head and stared at the lamp. Looking at the smooth, silver surface, I could now see the engravings of four animals, a moose, bear, panther, and eagle etched on the side.

The events of today were all so surreal. It started when Marcus told me about the legend of Goah, then I found the artifact, and now I was the center of the ceremony. I wasn't sure what was going on. It all felt like a dream.

The Prime Ministerial produced the cobalt bottle and held it up for all eyes to see. "Behold the first artifact."

He stood there while the room erupted in cheers and muttering between the Fetchers spread throughout the Great Hall.

"Good brothers . . ." shouted, The Prime Ministerial.

The room fell silent.

"This Fetcher comes before us as a brother who devoted himself to the creed and upheld his post with belief. For he believed, wholeheartedly, that he could find the relic of antiquity." He displayed it to the room moving his arm in an arch. "This relic represents the first value of our Fetcher's creed—Belief. Without belief, we have no reason to look for what we cannot find. Belief also means faith and fidelity to one's promise. It is the ability to stay true to your beliefs through the course of time." The Prime Ministerial placed the bottle on the table, then lifted the lamp with both hands. "Through this flame, burning true and constant, our brother, Fletcher Barnes believed in his duty and proved his belief."

The Prime Ministerial paused. He furrowed his brow as his pleasant nature turned to one of displeasure. He scowled down at me for what seemed like an eternity before setting the lamp on the table. Finally, he spoke again, "However . . . he also broke the Fetchers creed. Fletcher Barnes held onto the relic for his own intention. He failed the Ministerial in his job to present the relic of antiquity to guarantee the Ministerial's authority for all of time. Thus, he failed the brotherhood."

The room went uncomfortably silent.

"What say you brother, Barnes?"

"I . . . Er . . . I . . ."

I didn't know what to say. I knelt there with a giant frog in my throat, unable to formulate a reason why I had held on to the artifact. I didn't want to reveal that Marcus suggested I keep it hidden. I didn't want them to do anything to him.

"You will be judged for your transgression." He bent over and blew the flame of the lamp out. "As for the rest of you, it is your sworn duty to continue the search for the relics of antiquity. You will all be dispatched to new posts in the morning. Now, return to your chambers, for this will be the last night you spend in San Fargo."

The Prime Ministerial pointed at me. I stared at his fingertip. "You, don't go anywhere, your fate will be decided in our chambers." He signaled his guards, and two of them circled behind me. They each grabbed an arm, lifted me off the ground and carried me toward the doorway to the antechamber.

As I was whisked away, I caught Marcus's concerned look. I could tell he wanted to rush up and help, but I gave him a nod, feigned a smile, and silently mouthed

'IT'S OKAY.'
And then, he was out of sight.

THE FOUR CORNERSTONES

I was certain that was the last time I was going to see Marcus. Knowing I was headed to my end, tears streamed down my cheeks. I struggled against the rough hands that suspended me in the air, but the Ministerial Guards squeezed my biceps tighter, to the point my hands were numb. I quickly decided it was pointless to wiggle anymore, so I let them carry me into the antechamber. I lowered my head and cried.

The guards took me to the center of the room and let me go. When my feet touched the floor, I stood shaking, struggling to stand. My knees and legs trembled with fright, and my body shook with each silent sob. I didn't want to die.

A few moments later, I heard footsteps behind me, and I raised my head, held back the tears, and found the courage to face my fate. The Prime Ministerial circled around me and looked at me across the circular table I was now facing. I felt a presence appear at either side, and the Oraculum placed a single hand on each of my shoulders. Goosebumps formed on my skin and a shiver of fear ran down my spine.

Instantly, I remembered the day I became a Fetcher. I was six. It was the annual 'Day of Knowing' where all the six-year-olds in the nation were brought before the

Ministerial Court. I remembered standing in line, wondering what my chosen profession was going to be. Was I going to be a chef, street sweeper, or an entertainer? I approached the podium where the Oraculum were standing. They grabbed each other's hand, and each placed their free hand on my shoulders. As they faced me, I stared at the right Oraculum's marked face. The seer tranced me with his steel gray eyes and a cloud filled my mind as he searched through my memories. They released their grip from my shoulders and the other Oraculum, the doer, announced my fate.

"This one . . . Fletcher Barnes . . . will be a . . . FETCHER."

The Ministerial Guard had whisked me away from my parents. I was taken to San Fargo to live the life of a Fetcher. Next to today, that was the lowest day of my life. I didn't think life would get any worse than being taken from my parents at the age of six—but it had.

I came back to the present when the Oraculum squeezed my shoulders, just as the Prime Ministerial addressed me in his proper authoritative voice.

"Fletcher Barnes, what are we going to do with you?" he said, then paused. "On a high note, you found my first artifact. You deserve an accommodation and to be promoted to the highest level. Your efforts are worthy of a Hero. However, on a low note, you kept the artifact hidden from me, and my Guard. You broke the creed you solemnly swore to and broke the laws of this nation. Your actions are those of a thief, and thus should be punished as such."

There was silence in the room. All I heard was my broken breaths, in and out, and the ticking, of the clock, on the back wall. That is when I saw it. The large picture of a middle-aged man with clean-cut graying black hair hung on the wall and seemed to be looking at me over the Prime Ministerial's shoulder. The man's soft, brown eyes started at me from under his thin eyebrows, and I felt a sense of warmth coming from the subtle brushstrokes. As the warmth filled my body and my strength returned, I realized of the man on the canvas looked familiar. The cheekbones and kind eyes reminded me of Marcus. But there was something else about the picture that struck me. It also looked a lot like the Prime Ministerial.

"What say you?" asked the Prime Ministerial.

My gaze leapt from the picture back to his face. There was that question again. How was I going to answer it this time? I thought quickly.

"I knew it might be special; I didn't know what to do with it," I replied sheepishly. "I was going to turn it in."

The Prime Ministerial stared down his long nose at me. I could tell by his furrowed brow that he didn't believe me.

"You were going to keep it for yourself . . . weren't you?"

"No." I said, knowing it was a half-truth. I really hadn't known what I was going to do with it.

"You were, and now you will be judged—your fate is in the hands of the Oraculum."

My mind went foggy again and I felt the seer poking around in my mind. This time I fought mentally to keep them from seeing my thoughts from the day. Finally, he retreated, and the room came back into focus.

"What is your decision?" the Prime Ministerial asked the Oraculum.

The Oraculum on my left spoke up, "A Fetcher no more, he will be."

"And then?"

"Removed from all, he will become."

My heart sank. *Removed from all,* I thought. *That can't be good.*

"But wait . . . he is *the one.*"

The scorn on the Prime Ministerial's face evaporated. His brows raised and the light came back into his eyes, and a smile formed at the corners of his pursed lips.

"And so it will be," said the Prime Ministerial. He reached into his pocket and gently took out the bottle. He held it out for me to see the marking of the tree, and slowly, almost deliberately, lowered it.

My eyes followed the bottle as he placed it on the table next to a stone tablet. The tablet was slightly smaller than my dinner tray, but about an inch thick. The light-gray granite, with hues of pink and dark blue sprinkled throughout, had strange, chiseled markings—a diamond shaped hole in the middle, with four channels separating the tablet into four boxes. A single word: BELIEF, STRENGTH, COURAGE, and RESOLVE, was etched into the smooth surface of each box. I believed it had something to do with our creed.

Then I noticed the old, wrinkled scroll curled up around the corners of the tablet. It had yellowed over time but the markings on the paper were still distinct. My eyes scanned the picture. It looked like a map of some kind, and I wondered what it had to do with any of this. Then I saw a watermark on the corner of the paper. It was the same shape as the white tree on the face of the bottle I found.

The Artifacts. I thought. *The tablet and the map had to do with the artifacts.*

Trying not to show my excitement, I looked up at

the Prime Ministerial. A look of wanting showed through the seriousness on his face. It was as if he knew something, anticipated something.

He furrowed his brow and narrowed his eyes at me. His chilly stare permeated my soul. My shoulders shuddered as a coldness ran down my spine.

"Guards!" he called. "We are done with this Fetcher. Take him to his tower and lock him there until morning, when he will be transported to the prison in Gullet."

The Oraculum stepped around me and stood behind the Prime Ministerial with their backs to me. They looked up at the photo of the old man, as if they were paying homage to him. The two guards whisked me away.

Belief
Strensth
ourase
Resolve

THIN RAY OF LIGHT

Excitement ran through my veins. I couldn't stand it any longer. I had to sneak back to the antechamber. First, I had to get out of my locked room. I walked over to my wardrobe, threw on a clean shirt, took out my leather satchel, flung it over my shoulder, slipped on my sandals, and walked back to the window.

I looked over my window ledge and peered down at the window below. It was cracked open. The old man on the second floor had passed away a few weeks ago and they were airing it out. No one had moved in yet, and the Ministerial Guards had not checked the windows. It was a perfect escape route. I moved to my bed and stripped it down. I took the top blanket, ripped it into long strips and tied them all together. I anchored it to the wooden frame of the bed then ripped the sheets into strips. I tied them to the end of the blanket and tugged it tight making sure it would hold my weight.

Satisfied, I stepped onto the edge of the window, scanned the city wall for guards—of which there were none—and threw the sheets over. They were just long enough. I could see the fabric dangling halfway down the open window, the corner gently tapping against the windowpane.

Standing on the ledge, I held the rough fabric in my

hands. My heart pounded in my chest, hoping that the bed would hold my weight. I wasn't worried about it moving, as the top of the frame was bolted to the wall. I was more concerned about the leg breaking off or the fabric ripping—there were many holes in it from years of wear. Leaning back, I told myself not to look down, but I did anyway. Immediately, I felt as if the ground was rushing up to meet me; my head spun, but I didn't let go. I faced forward and closed my eyes, regaining my senses.

"Here we go," I whispered softly, and rappelled backwards.

My hands gripped the sheets as my feet searched for purchase along the stone wall of the tower. Slowly, I inched my way down to the second-floor window. I reached the top of the window and carefully placed my feet on the wooden frame. I pushed inward, hoping to widen the opening, but the window would not move. Then, I remembered the first time I had tried opening my window. The sunlight had heated up the ten layers of oily paint, causing it to stick to the casing, sealing it in its place.

Faced with two choices, I decided I didn't want to climb back to my room—besides my arms were already burning and my hands were aching from gripping the sheets so tightly. I had to swing out and push on the window frame. I took a deep breath and counted down.

"Three . . ."

"Two . . ."

"One!"

I pushed off, swinging out over the road. The knot slipped.

"Oh, Shoooot . . ." I blurted out as I hit the window frames with my feet.

The knot came apart. Seconds later, pain radiated

from the side of my head, along my right side, down to my knees. I lay there unmoving, wondering if I had fallen to my death, when I realized it was dark all around me. I was in the room.

I sat up, rubbed the back of my head where it had hit the windowsill, and dizzily stood up. I stepped over to the window and pulled the sheet, which hung lifeless over the sill, into the room. I realized I was lucky. I had managed to keep my feet together, hitting the window frame where the windows parted. The window gave, and I landed with a huge thump on the ground as my momentum carried me forward. if not for this lucky streak of fortune, I would have hit the glass, or fallen to my death twenty-five feet below.

I stayed in the room for a minute, wondering if the guards had heard the noise, but no one came. I walked over to the door, slid the latch, and slowly pulled it open enough for me to slip through. The stairwell was dark, and there was no movement within it. Realizing I was safe, I slipped down the stairs and crept through the streets, stealthily slinking in the shadows of every barrel, cart, or doorway I could find, making sure that I kept out of the sight of the guards patrolling on the wall. I made my way down to the Great Hall and quietly entered through the main door into the dining room.

Hiding against the interior wall, I studied the room, making out the dull shapes of the long tables and benches laid out before me. A single guard sat against the far wall. By his outline, I could see he was slumped down in his chair, and the soft rumble of his snoring echoed throughout the hall, telling me he was asleep.

I was in the clear if I didn't wake him. I followed the far wall around the guard almost tripping over his outstretched feet. I had not seen those in the shadows. I was angry at myself for almost ruining my chances of getting to the chamber. I stood over the guard as his deep snores reverberated through the open space. Slowly, I reached down to his laces, pulled them out and tied all four ends together in a huge knot.

My pulse racing, I inched my way down the hall to the massive oak door leading to the antechamber. I slowly slid the latch, only a slight click sounded through the hall. I moved inside and closed the door behind me drawing the latch shut. I knew I was safe when I still heard the guard's snores through the door.

The room was dark. Long, thick drapes were pulled across the windows and the only light that came in was a tiny sliver of moonlight from one of the cracks between the drapes. Trying to remember the layout of the room, I sidestepped a large chair to my right and stepped forward to the table. My eyes now adjusted to the faint light, I saw that the tablet and the map were still there.

Stepping up to the tablet, I looked down, and placed my fingers on the word inscribed on the top left corner. "BELIEF." I noticed the other three words inscribed on the other corners of the tablet; "STRENGTH", "COURAGE", "RESOLVE." I knew instantly where the Fetcher's creed came from. I read the smaller inscription below the word BELIEF.

For the unseen believed in, is proof of something.
Something of belief is also confidence.
Trust, loyalty, and actions, of duty,
Speak loud in standards of merit and truth.
Intangible, conviction is action.
Trust in it and go forward with BELIEF.

Remembering the lamp of belief earlier in the night, and now seeing this inscription, I realized this was a sign that I was supposed to be here, taking the tablet, and searching for the other artifacts myself.

Suddenly, an uneasy feeling washed over me. I felt their presence. It was the Oraculum. Were they watching me? I looked around the room, but no one was there. Another wave of unease washed over me, and I knew I had to get out of there.

I picked up the heavy tablet and placed it in my satchel. It barely fit.

As I picked up the scroll, I realized it was made of a canvas-like material, instead of parchment, as I had thought earlier. I quickly scanned the drawings, and realized it was a map of our country. There were four markings on it. Spread out in each of the corners of the continent there was a drawing of a city; in the apace of San Fargo, there were caves near the top, a volcano near the bottom and off to the side, was a picture of tall peaks in the mountain range. The uneasy feeling getting stronger, I quickly rolled up the map and placed it in my bag with the tablet.

Reaching for the bottle, I stopped. "Thank you," I said staring into Lorucias Guifachs face of the painting over the mantle and took the bottle. I placed it in the pocket on my bag and buttoned the flap, securing it inside.

I wasn't sure where I was going to go next, but I felt an urge to flee—to go far away from this place. First, however, I had to get out of here alive. The Ministerial would have my hide for taking these things.

It tired the latch on the door, and to my surprise, it was not locked. I made my way out of the room, careful not to disturb anything and poked my head around the corner. They leaned against the wall. I heard the guards snoring and I knew I could potentially escape.

Adrenaline pumping, I crept over to where they sat with their legs straight out in front of them. Their heads bobbed up and down as they snored. I carefully tied their bootlaces together.

One of them opened their eyes as his own snore woke him up and looked straight into mine.

"Bob, wake up!" he shouted. "The Fetcher is escaping."

I ran.

THE ESCAPE

I half expected the Ministerial guard to grab me, but my brilliant lace-job caused him to stumble and knee the other guard in the head, knocking him out cold. Then I saw the heavy man fall forward. His face hit the bench of the table before him snapping his head backward.

I knew I was safe, for now, but I carefully exited through the main door in case there were other guards stationed outside. I checked my surroundings and darted across the street to hide in the shadow of the row of barracks that loomed over me.

Slowly, I inched myself along the barracks. When I reached the corner, I spied the outer city wall. It was empty. I figured I had just enough time to make it down the incline, to the base of the wall, before any guards came around.

I took several steadying breaths to calm my nerves, placed my hand on the satchel to steady it, and made a mad dash. Flying past several rows of houses and shop fronts, I made the wall in no time flat and stood there with my back against the cold sandstone wall.

I was on the southwest side of San Fargo. The gate was just to the north and a bit more to the west of me. There was no way I was going to get out of the city that way. It took the gatekeeper to unlock the gate, and several guards to unroll the chains and lower the drawbridge across the river. I realized I was in a predicament. I was stuck. I hadn't thought this through. I had no way to escape the city.

Just then, a memory from a year ago flashed through my mind. Marcus and I were on a walk around the perimeter of the city. He pointed out a small, wooden access door that had been bolted and chained shut. At the time, I wondered why he would show me such a thing. Leaving the city was the last thing on my mind then, but now I understood why—he had known this day was coming.

I padded along the cobblestone road and made my way toward the access door. When I reached the door, I noticed the chain had been cut, and was hanging lifeless from the hook on the wall.

I glanced around, making sure no one had followed me, slid my fingers into the gap between the splintered wood and the rough edges of the sandstone, and pulled. The door did not budge. I pulled harder. The rusted hinges screamed fiercely, penetrating the night air. This time the door opened a foot—and stopped.

I was afraid I had given away my position at the wall, but no one came. I pulled at the door again. The hinges creaked louder but it gave me enough room to slip into the small passageway. I stood in the dark, breathing easy, knowing I was almost out of the city. A slight breeze blew into the tunnel, carrying the sweet smell of the meadow and the damp mist of the river.

I walked toward the moonlight at the end of the passageway and came to a small stairway that led down to the riverbank. I checked the city wall above and behind me, descended the small flight of stairs, and stepped onto the soft gray mud.

I was free. Then it hit me. *How am I going to get across the river?*

That's when I saw him. A man sitting at the edge of the river with his back towards me.

He wasn't there a few minutes ago—or was he?

Sandals next to him, his feet in the water, the man turned to look at me. "What are you doing here?" he said softly and grinned as if he already knew the answer to his question.

I realized it was Marcus. I hadn't recognized him in the moonlight.

"What are *you* doing here?" I asked him, as I stepped up next to him.

"Reflecting," he said softly, and smiled again. "I had to be here tonight."

"Another one of your dreams?"

"Yeah." Marcus stood up and placed a warm hand on my shoulder. "I sneak out here occasionally. I enjoy the feeling of the crisp cold water rushing over my toes when I tip my feet in the water. So, I sit, and dip, and stare at the shadows in the meadow."

We stood there in silence for a moment, taking in the peace of the night, smelling the scents of the wildflowers, and appreciating the radiance of the moonlight.

"Go ahead . . . see what I mean . . . put your feet in the water," Marcus said, breaking the silence. "It will change your life."

I didn't see how putting my feet in the river would change my life.

"Go on," he urged.

"Sure, all right," I said, and stepped in with my sandals on. The sensation of the ice-cold water running over my feet was amazing. Shivers ran up and down my spine and added to the pull of the full moon—I felt excitement run through my veins.

"I saw this night coming," he said, in his soft, raspy voice. "When I woke up this morning, I knew today was the day everything was going to change for us."

I looked up at Marcus. A mischievous look danced on his face.

"Sometimes I stand here wondering what would happen if I were to jump in." he said changing the subject. "You know . . . I guess everyone needs a little nudge occasionally."

Before the words cold sink through the walls of my thick skull, Marcus slid his hand off my shoulder, down to the middle of my back, then, pushed me in—as if all of this was some great plan of his.

MY WORST FEAR

There was nothing I could do to catch myself as I fell face first into the river. I tried to scream Marcus's name, but the cool water rushed into my mouth, turning my words into a garble that sounded something like, *"Magooosh."* My body, shocked by the ice-cold water, and heavy from the tablet that pulled at my shoulder, was dragging down to the soft gray bottom.

My feet sunk into the goo at the bottom of the river. The rushing water yearned to free me and sweep me out to sea. I held tight to my satchel and kicked off the bottom. My feet stuck. I pushed off and wiggled my feet free.

My head broke the surface a few feet away from where Marcus stood. I saw his silhouette out of the corner of my eye as the current drug me away. I kicked with all my might, even as many forces worked against me. The waters churned around my head, splashing into my mouth making it difficult to gather breath; the stone tablet tugged at my shoulder, urging me to the bottom; and the river swept me violently past the city wall towards the jagged cliffs of the ravine that led out to sea.

I knew this was my only chance to make it to the edge. I swam hard, trying to keep my head above water and stroke towards land. As I neared the bank, the unseen forces kept working against me. The weight of the tablet drained my energy, while the current pushed me in the opposite direction. I believed that the icy water didn't want to lose its grip on me, and I was losing the battle. Where the river turned and headed in towards the cliffs, I was pulled away from the bank. I saw the muddy gray shore receding further and further out of sight. It was like a bad dream. The one where you want something, you get close to it, and then it is slowly pulled away from you until you can't see it anymore.

The water became more violent, and the satchel felt heavier. A wave splashed in my face, I breathed in the cool liquid, and panicked as and my head sank under the water. My arms flailed as I tried to gather breath, but only water filled my lungs.

Drowning was my worst fear. Here I was . . . I was drowning now. I gave up and let the water take me. I was done for—a goner.

Curious, drowning was more peaceful than I had thought. With my mouth blocked, and my throat filled with water, my mind cleared, and my body went limp. The sound of rushing water filled my ears, and darkness consumed me taking me to a far-off place.

CHEATING DEATH

I felt a tug on my shoulder, then I was being lifted. *Is this what it is like to be dead? Am I being pulled into the afterlife?* I didn't know what was happening to me. I came to rest on a soft bed. Then, something nudged me in the side and pushed against my ribs.

Stop it! I thought, annoyed at the jabbing.

I was at peace and wanted to be left alone—to die.

Then something nudged me again, and again.

As I was ripped out of the grip of death, my senses flooded back to me. I was aware that I was lying on my side. My left arm was twisted up underneath me at a weird angle and my head rested on something hard. It didn't feel right. I always imagined Heaven would be all soft and fluffy—nothing hard. I felt the weight of the satchel on my hip, my head pounded, my lungs ached, and shades of gray spread out before me. I was on the riverbank.

My body shook violently as I spewed water, like a fountain, out of my mouth. I rolled over, pulled myself to my hands and knees, coughed, and gagged, for what seemed like an eternity. When I finally got enough air into my lungs that I thought I was doing well, I vomited my dinner; half-choking on chewed up green beans, potatoes, and steak.

My nose and throat burned, but finally, I was able to breathe regularly without water or vomit getting in the way. Then I saw it. Next to my hands, sunk into the mud, were two giant hooves.

I froze, not knowing what to do. Slowly I leaned backwards, looking at the chest of a giant hairy beast. I had cheated death, but now a monster towered over me.

THE SPIRIT OF THE WOLF

Have you ever stared up the nose of a Moose? I hadn't either, until this day. Two big nostrils flared in front of my face as the animal lowered its head and stared at me. Staring back at it, I felt its warm breaths blow over my cheeks, through my eyebrows, and over my wet hair. Frozen to my spot, I looked past the massive, curved snout, and looked up, into the beast's beady, black eyes. I didn't know whether I should run or jump back into the water. Then I realized it must have been Moose that pulled me out of the water, and I relaxed a bit.

"We need to get moving," said a gruff, masculine voice.

I looked to my right, through the massive horns, and saw my wolf standing there looking up at me.

"Don't just stand there . . . we need to get into the forest before someone sees you."

I stared at Wolf. I couldn't believe it at first, but when I heard the voice and saw its lips moving at the same time, I couldn't deny that it was really talking to me. I shook my head, trying to get the remnants of water out of my ears, when he spoke again.

"Come on Nalfgar, this one is dense," Wolf said then turned around.

Moose stared at me, blinked, and for a second I

thought I could see it smile at me, before turning, and following Wolf to the edge of the forest.

I pinched my arm, thinking I was dead or dreaming, but, as I felt the sting, I had to accept that this was not a dream—I was surely alive.

"Wait . . . did you just talk . . . and did that moose just smile at me?" I asked, as I picked my satchel up off the mud and started after the animals.

Wolf did not respond, but I thought I saw Moose lifting its head up and down as if it were nodding in affirmation to my question. I followed them to the edge of the forest and paused as I felt the Douglas Firs looming over me, and a great magnetism pulled at me from deep within the forest.

The animals disappeared amongst the huckleberry bushes, and I took a deep breath to prepare myself before I followed them down the game path. Immediately, I felt the temperature change, and the cool mist of the forest, the fresh smell of moss and decaying leaves and nettles tantalized my senses.

We hiked easily over several rises where the scenery changed. I stopped in awe at what I saw: The majestic moonlight filtered through the branches of the massive Redwoods; reflected off the dew that collected on the thousands of leaves of the ferns covering the ground, illuminating them like millions of diamonds. It was a sight that penetrated my soul, spreading warmth throughout my body. Right there, right then, I knew what it felt like to really be "alive."

The sound of marbled murrelets flying to their mossy nests above pulled me out of my trance, and I saw Wolf and Moose standing in the middle of the valley waiting for me. I followed them, all the while staring at the wonders around me, listening to the calls, squeaks, and noises from the murrelets, squirrels, and elk that occupied this part of the forest.

I was amazed by the splendor of the forest.

"He is caught by the forest," Moose grunted.

"Yes, he is feeling its power," Wolf responded.

"It is so beautiful," I replied. "I have never been in a forest before, let alone one so beautiful."

"We are only on the edge of the great Macho-Nilo Forest, there are many more wonders inside it, but we must go in a different direction."

That was the last time they spoke to me for several hours. We kept to the trail along the edge of the Macho-Nilo Forest. Just as I felt that my feet were going to fall off, we stopped. I followed Wolf and Moose as they veered off the path, cut through some bushes and after a few hundred yards, came to a small clearing.

"We will rest here," Moose said, and pointed his antlers at a log that had fallen near the edge of the perimeter.

I plopped down on the decaying tree trunk and picked out of my heel, the splinter that had been incessantly digging in for the last mile or so. When I looked up, Wolf was gone and Moose was lying down near me, his feet curled up under his hulky body. It stared at me with inquisitive eyes.

Neither of us moved, until few moments later, a man emerged from the underbrush. Startled, I jumped up, prepared to run—where I didn't know. I guess I would just run into the woods.

"Firewood anyone?" a deep voice said, plopping a pile of twigs and branches onto the ground between Moose and me.

Recognizing the voice, I sat down and watched in wonder as the stranger assembled the firewood in the pit that was hiding at the end of the log. The figure before me was not Wolf I had come with, although its voice was the same. He was an older man, with long silver hair that flowed out from underneath a wolf head he wore as a hat. The wolf head was attached to a pelt that covered his back and hung down past his waist. It was the only thing covering him bar a small loincloth covering his privates. The front legs of the pelt draped over his shoulders—the claws hung past his chest—and the legs dangled in the dirt as he crouched there barefooted in front of the fire pit. The markings on the fur were the same as those on Wolf I had come to know during my years in San Fargo. The man was thin as a rail, yet his muscles were clearly defined underneath his wrinkly, tanned skin. I watched him diligently work at stacking the branches just right. With a quick flick of the wrist, a spark shot out of his fingers and ignited the dried moss at the base.

Then he stood up and swiftly moved towards the log. His movements were stealthy and precise, and with the pelt on he looked just like a wolf. *Is he a wolf, or is he a man?* My eyes were playing tricks on me. As he neared the log, I saw several tattoos on his body, one on each bicep, and one on each thigh. Each showed one was one of the animals Marcus had told me about, the same ones that were etched on the silver lamp at the ceremony.

"You must be wondering who I am?" the man said, sitting down next to me.

"Er . . . yeah."

"My name is Wasgo. I am a Weiorweijaoj."

"A Werewolf?"

"In a sense. I am a sprit wolf . . . a shape shifter . . . and I am your spirit guide."

"Someone pinch me!" I said, looking around for someone to wake me from this strange dream.

"Fletcher—this is real."

"You know my name?"

"I know a lot of things. However, all will be explained in due time."

"Hold on a second . . . you were a wolf a few minutes ago . . . a talking wolf, with a talking moose friend, of course . . . and now you are a man. Please explain *that* to me?"

"I am your spirit protector . . ."

"I know, you just said that."

Wasgo pursed his lips, furrowed his brow, and held his hand up to silence me. "I am half man, half wolf. You, Fletcher, are destined for something great—greater than you know—and I was sent here to help you, guide you, on your journey."

I looked down at the moose tattoo on his right bicep. "Wait a minute, does all of this have anything to do with the story about Goah."

"'Tis not a story."

His amber eyes stared at me, holding all sincerity in the world, and I realized that there was something more going on here than I knew about.

"Let me explain," he said, a smile forming on his black lips.

I looked upon him intently, waiting for answers. Although he looked human, he also looked very much like a wolf, with eyes slightly slanted, a triangular face, and a nose that jutted out, moving ever so slightly as he breathed in and out.

"Many years ago, I was born to Stagarth and Hallowa, two wolves that lived deep within these woods. As I grew, I began to feel different, like I was meant to be something other than an ordinary wolf. One day when Stagarth and I were hunting, we came across a tree. Now, this was not your ordinary tree. It was the great tree of life."

"The one on the bottle," I said.

"Mmm, yes."

I reached into the pocket of my satchel, pulled out the cobalt bottle, and ran my finger over the white tree as he continued.

"My father feared the tree and would not go close to it. I, on the other hand, was drawn to it. I sat down before it and looked up into its great branches. After a moment, a figure appeared before me. He was a majestic and mystic cloud before my eyes. He reached out and touched my nose, and before I knew it, I transformed into a man. Then he touched my temple, and, in an instant, I knew everything I needed to know about the legend, the artifacts, and you. What came next surprised me. Goah gave me a choice. I could accept his gift and be a part of something greater or go on being a wolf."

"Let me guess . . ."

"I left my family and my ordinary life to help you."

"Why?"

"Let me explain some more and maybe you will understand." Wasgo paused and reflected for a moment. "Lorucias Guifachs was a middle-aged man of pleasing personality, well-liked by his community, and lived in an old house that was passed down to him through several generations. His family, when they founded the town of Gullett, was the first to build on the site of an ancient ruin.

"Now Lorucias Guifachs was an ordinary man, with limited experience of the world and not so much as a talent to his name, but for collecting things. He was a man of nature and kept a wolf as his pet.

"One day, while sifting through his collection of

antiquities in his attic, he was bitten by a spider. Now, the venom of this spider did not administer immediate death. No, it was a rather slow working toxin that affected the nerves.

"Over the course of a week, he became increasingly mentally disturbed, and began wandering through the streets of Gullet. Many thought he was crazy—spouting insane nonsense about moose, panthers, bears, and eagles.

"Then, on this night, fifty-two years ago, he set fire to his house and stood there with his arms stretched out ordering the Fire Brigade not to interfere with his purpose as he watched it burn to the ground. After first arresting him, the authorities found him innocent for the law stated that a man can do whatever he wishes with his possessions. If he wanted to burn his house, he could do so if it didn't affect anyone or anything else.

"That next night, Lorucias Guifachs was sifting through the ashes when he found a secret passage that had been previously hidden by the floor of the house. Burning the house down was the only way he could have found it. He lifted the great stone covering the entrance and followed the passageway as it led underneath the city to a small chamber. There, he found a message that he was to search for four artifacts hidden throughout the land. The message also told him that the artifacts would greatly benefit humanity, and it was imperative for him to find them."

I looked at Wasgo in disbelief, wondering if all of this was some strange hoax.

"I sense you don't believe me."

I stood up to pace around the clearing, then stopped at the fire. "This is just really hard to believe."

"I know how you feel but let me assure you that all

of this is all real.”

“How can this be real? I mean, you are a shape shifting wolf, and he is a talking moose.”

“Oi! Not just any old moose,” the moose said, lifting his head. “I am the great Nalfgar, protector of the water relic, savior of your hide!”

“Easy Nalfgar, he has been through a lot today—he is in shock from all of this, as we all were at first.”

Nalfgar snorted, then lowered his head and closed his eyes.

“This is real . . . because I was there that night.”

I turned away from the fire and stared into Wasgo’s eyes.

“It was I who led Lorucias down the tunnel,” he said softly. “I showed him his destiny—the tablet you hold in your hands—and told him about the relics.”

“That’s impossible.” I said with disbelief. “That would make you...”

“Over fifty-two years old,” Wasgo replied. “And now here we are.”

“Yeah well, some of us had a choice in all of this. At least you knew what was in store for you.”

“You are right,” Wasgo said. He stood and walked over to me and placed a hand on my shoulder. “I did have a choice, and so do you. Get some rest and maybe it will be clearer in the morning.”

Wasgo lay down near the fire, curled up on his side, pulled the pelt over his body and went to sleep.

I lay down with my head propped up against the log and watched the sleeping animals. When the fire died, the clearing grew dark, and my thoughts ran wild. *What if I don’t want to do this? What if my choice is to go back to San Fargo?*

My mind scurried around in circles, processing the

events from the day, and wondering about what lay ahead. Sometime, during the night, it became clear to me that I did have a choice. I could go back now, but really, I must do this—I was chosen for this task. Finally, my brain quieted, and I fell into a deep sleep.

THE MINES OF ETONIA

I shot straight out of my dream state and sat upright. After I gathered my wits about me, I realized I was once again in the clearing, sitting near the log. Nalfgar was across the way munching on the branches of a nearby tree, and Wasgo was roasting a small animal over the fire.

"Come eat," Wasgo said, holding up the roasted rabbit. "We need to get moving."

I met Wasgo at the fire where he handed me a slice of hot meat. Blowing on it, I took a bite and swallowed. The juicy, oily rabbit satisfied my grumbling, empty stomach.

Wasgo smiled at me, took a huge bite out of the rabbit leg he was holding and let the rabbit juice dribble down his chin. *Even though he looks like a man, he still eats like an animal.* I thought and picked some more meat off the carcass.

Just as we finished our meal, Nalfgar lumbered over to the fire and peed on it, dousing the hot coals. I plugged my nose blocking the burnt acidic smell as Wasgo scooped some dirt onto the pit and tamped it with his foot.

I followed Nalfgar through the underbrush as we made our way back to the trail. Wasgo followed behind me, and when I stepped out of the trees, he had morphed back into his wolf body.

"We can travel quicker if you ride on Nalfgar."

I stepped on Wasgo's back and climbed onto the moos's back and we set off. After a while I settled into the rhythm of his movements, and it thrilled me to think that I was actually riding on the back of a moose. Marcus wouldn't believe it.

Wasgo sprinted ahead of us to scout the trail. Every now and again, he would come into sight then dash ahead. After a day's worth of traveling, we finally neared our destination. Wasgo stopped in the middle of the trail. His ears stood at attention, his tail shot straight out, and his snout moved about as he sniffed the air.

"We are near the camp," he said, as Nalfgar came to a halt behind him. "It is over the rise, to the right. I can smell hundreds of them—we must keep our distance for now."

Wasgo turned and headed into the trees to our left. Nalfgar and I followed. We remained hidden in the trees as we circled around the left side of the camp. Every now and again, I would catch glimpses of the gray miners' tents and the washing that was strung out between camps. It wasn't hard to miss the gray shirts with the ruby Fs on them.

My friends and I stopped behind two trees. One had fallen over, propped against the other, making a natural lean-to that not only hid our position perfectly, but also gave us a straight line of sight of the west side of the camp.

Women and children were busy preparing meals as the men returned from the mines carrying their large hammers and pickaxes. Sweat glistened off their chest and backs as the late afternoon sun filtered through the tree branches. In exchange for their mining tool, each man was greeted by his woman with a fresh shirt to wear, and kiss on the cheek.

Just then, a Ministerail Guard on patrol rode by on his horse. He scouted the perimeter of the camp, one hand on the reins, his other hand on the hilt of his sword, ready to pounce on any Fetcher who tried to escape. I counted the seconds until the next patrol passed by.

"Two minutes between guards," I told Wasgo.

"Good, that gives you enough time to sneak into camp."

"This is where I leave you," said Nalfgar. "Good luck Fletcher!" He nodded at me.

"You have done your part, my friend," said Wasgo. "May good fortune find you wherever you go."

Nalfgar nodded at Wasgo. "And you, my friend." The giant animal turned and disappeared into the trees, heading away in the opposite direction from which came.

Sneak into camp. What Wasgo had said a minute before finally sank into my head, and I turned to face him. "You want me to sneak into camp? If I go in there, I am going to get caught!"

"What is the next artifact?"

I thought about the legend.

"I don't know, but I know it is not in there," I said and pointed to camp.

"Pull out your tablet," Wasgo commanded.,

I pulled the stone tablet out of my satchel. It was heavy in my hands. I laid it flat on the ground and studied the face. It was the first opportunity I had had to examine the tablet. The light gray granite had small amber letters set into the surface.

The top right corner of the tablet had the words "BELIEF" inscribed into it. I read the inscription again and thought about what Goah had said to me on the cloud. He was right. I observed my belief. I had dived almost every day while searching for an artifact that nobody had ever seen. They didn't even know where it was, or even if it was real. Through my own belief, and the belief in my fellow Fetchers, I carried out my oath, finding the glass bottle in the process.

I moved my fingers across to the top left quarter of the tablet and traced out the word "STRENGTH", then read the words below it.

There is strength in one, and one strength in all.
The body is strong the mind is stronger.
Add to that the mindful might of spirit,
The force of three exert their power more.
Like water and wind, persistence erodes.
Encourage it and go forward with STRENGTH.

"What do you think the next artifact is," Wasgo asked.

I thought of strength. I looked past the camp and saw the hill that held with the mouth of the mine in the distance. "A rock," I replied.

"Not just any rock," said Wasgo.

"A diamond."

"Right, a diamond," he reiterated. "How else are you going to find it, if you don't go into that camp?"

I looked into Wasgo's eyes. They were serious. I knew he was right.

"I'll be right here if you need me. Everything will be all right," he said, trying to reassure me.

As I looked into his eyes, I wanted to believe him. What Marcus had said on the boat the day before popped into my head, "If fear takes hold, it replaces everything."

I swallowed, trying to wash away the lump in my throat with saliva. There it was again. I was afraid. Fear had its hold on me. I looked back down at the tablet and ran my fingers over the last sentence: "Go forward in STRENGTH." I realized that strength would replace my fear—It was up to me which one I chose.

I placed the tablet back in my pouch and crouched down to poke my head around the leaning tree trunk, waiting for the patrol. As soon as the guard rode his horse past and disappeared behind the tent, I ran for all I was worth.

ZION JOHNSON

I reached the nearest tent undetected. I pulled up the canvas peered underneath it, saw that it was safe, and slipped inside. My eyes adjusted to the dim light, and I stepped into the center of the tent and made my way to the front flaps, to survey the camp and figure out my next move.

As I neared the opening, the flap flew open and a girl about my age stepped into the tent and walked straight into me almost knocking me over. Startled, she opened her mouth to scream. I quickly placed my hand over her mouth and put my finger up to mine to silence her. She appeared terrified.

"Don't scream," I said, "I'm a Fetcher like you."

I lowered my finger, from my mouth to my chest, and pointed to the F on my shirt. I slowly removed my other hand from her mouth. I still saw the fear in her eyes.

"What do you want?"

I didn't know how to answer that. Whatever I told her would sound unbelievable. So, I decided to tell her the truth anyway.

"I am a Fetcher from San Fargo," I began. "I found the first artifact."

She stared at me unbelievingly, as if to say, "Yeah

right." She took a step backward and ran out of the tent.

I heard her shout as she ran, "Papa! Papa!" From the crack between the two flaps of canvas, I watched her run to a group of men standing before the campfire. She was talking to the largest man of the group, pointing back at the tent.

She began walking in my direction, hand-in-hand with the large man. When I saw the man fully, I froze, panicked. He lumbered towards me in his trousers and massive boots. He was the most muscular man I had seen in my life. His chest muscles bulged, and his biceps were bigger than my thigh. His head was completely shaven. On his face, he wore a short scraggly beard that followed his chiseled jawline emphasized his angular chin. His steel blue eyes, hiding behind prominent cheekbones, zeroed in on the mouth of the tent as he approached.

If I moved quickly, I could slip under the tent and make it back to the woods. Then I remembered the guard. It was about time for him to come back around and would not be good if I was caught. I would have to face this man—it was my better chance.

I shuffled backwards to the center of the tent, waiting for the man to enter.

His dark bald head came through first, his massive body following as he thumped into the room with his enormous boots. When he stood to full height, he almost touched the roof. I thought he must have been at least six foot eight, or so.

He came at me, then stopped. We were toe-to-toe, my neck cranked back to look into the whites of his eyes.

"My daughter, Alisa, says you have come from San Fargo."

That's a pretty name. It was the first thing that went

through my mind. I tried to answer him, but I was still paralyzed with fear. The words simply would not pass my lips.

He grabbed my shirt with a single fist and lifted me off the ground, so we were face-to-face.

"Answer me," he growled. "Are you from San Fargo?"

I nodded affirmatively.

"Great, Goah!" he said, and dropped me.

I almost fell on my backside but managed to stay on my feet by flapping my arms like a crow. I watched the man pace the room, rubbing his hand on his smooth head saying, "I don't believe it's true . . . It's happening . . . . It's time!"

Then he came over to me and kneeled on one knee. "Alisa said you found the first article. Is it here—is it with you?"

"Er . . . yes," I said, as I patted my satchel.

"Can I see it?" he asked.

I hesitated, wondering if he would take it and give it to the Ministerial Guard if I showed it to him.

"Please, I need to see with my own eyes that the legend is true," he pleaded.

I pulled the cobalt bottle out and held it up for him to see. The brute of a man almost melted in front of me. He held his hands out as if to caress the bottle but stopped an inch short and just stared at it in amazement.

"Great Goah . . . it's true!" He cupped my hands, holding me firmly, completely covering the bottle and all and held me firmly. "My name is Zion Johnson; I have devoted my life to finding an article such as this. You must protect this at all costs. I will help you."

"I am here for the second artifact," I replied.

"I know."

"Do you know where it is?"

"Yes, we have found it, but we cannot get to it."

"Will you show me?"

"In the morning," he said, his blue eyes sparkling like two sapphires. "Come, we must fill our stomachs: it is going to be a late night—we have planning to do!"

I put the bottle back in the pocket of my bag and followed him out of the tent. I passed Alisa, who was standing right outside the door. She must have heard everything. She looked at me with admiration, and as I passed, she grabbed my hand and walked with me to the campfire where a hundred or so men, women and children stood, waiting to receive me.

THE GREAT PANTHER

The fire snapped and spit at Zion as he stood in front of the pit. Illuminated by the flames, he recounted the story of The Great Panther.

"My father was the first one ever to arrive at this camp. He came here with the first group of Fetchers to mine the land in search of the artifact of the earth. He told me the story of Panther, the protector of the northern artifact and how he fought it off and beat it. I didn't believe him until about twenty years ago, my father was lost in a cave-in down in the mine. That night something quite strange, yet amazing happened right on this very spot."

Zion paused and grew bigger against the firelight. "I 'member it like it was yesterday. I sat by the fire and ate my dried meat, mourning my father. I was just twenty years old and lost without him." Zion paced in front of the fire, reflecting. "The other Fetchers were asleep in their tents. It was around midnight when I had this strange feeling that I was being watched. I threw a few more logs onto the fire and decided to sleep near the flames in case anything drew near in the night."

"I was drifting off when I heard the roars and screams near the mountain. I grabbed a torch, lit it, and ran to the guard's tent to see what had happened. They were all dead, mauled by some fierce animal."

"I ran back to my fire and stood near the flames, ready to protect the other Fetchers who were startled awake," he said, boldly. "Then it jumped out at me from the darkness. A giant Black Panther—twice my size—stood where you sit." Zion pointed at me. "I told the other Fetchers to stand back. And there I was, face to face with Panther. It was prowling back and forth in front of me, eyeing me like I was his lunch. Then it spoke to me."

"I am here to *protect* this mountain," it said.

"I am here to protect the Fetchers and *mine* this mountain," I replied.

"Then I must do what I must do like the guards," it said. "Its muscles twitched . . . tensed . . . and then it pounced!"

Zion stood in front of the fire at full height, his arms outstretched, and his fingers spread like a big cat's claws.

"I stood my ground and held my torch firmly. I was prepared to shove it in his mouth, and try to get away, but something strange happened. The flames in the pit grew and swirled then circled within a foot from me, creating a great barrier. Panther hit the flames and rolled to the ground in a smoldering heap."

Zion imitated Panther, rolling to the ground in front of the fire. He stood up and looked down at the spot where he had just lay.

"As quickly as the flames appeared, they were gone. I had no clue what had happened, I remember staring at Panther on the ground looking up at me with fearful eyes and thinking "This great beast is afraid of me." I walked over to it and patted out the smoldering bits on his back, and he . . . began to purr."

"After a minute, Panther sat up. He told me the

legend of Goah, as I am aware you *all* know by now—
and he told me something more." Zion looked me in the
eye and smiled. "Panther said I was chosen by Goah, and
that was why the fire stopped him. He told me I was to
prepare for the one to come: the one bearing the world
tree. Then Panther told me that the world-tree bearer
would also be the one to set us all free."

The group cheered. Zion sat down next to me. I
looked up at him, even sitting down he towered over me.

"I am here to help you in any way I can," he said
sincerely.

"Thank you," I said and sat in silence taking it all in.

After a while, I was feeling rather sleepy, so I left
Zion with the group of men and made my way to the
tent. I investigated the forest and met the amber eyes that
watched me, and I smiled. I didn't know how I was going
to find the remaining artifacts, but now I knew that I was
not alone. I had help.

I lay in the tent listening to the joyful celebrations
around camp. I felt a new, crushing weight on my soul. I
could hardly believe that I would be the one to find the
relics, let alone set everyone free.

A LESSON OF STRENGTH

Zion snored like a bear, and I had had a hard time getting comfortable on the cot. I lay there for what seemed like an eternity, thinking about the next artifact. Finally, the camp stirred, Alisa brought in a pail of fresh water and let me be the first to wash my face. I felt a little uncomfortable—she would not stop staring at me.

Her soft brown eyes followed me everywhere. The night before, she had watched me eat. She had watched me sitting with her father as we formed the plan to sneak me in and out of the mine. She had even taken the cot next to me and lay on her side, watching me until she fell asleep. Today, she had watched me wash, and now she stared me down while I ate my porridge. Despite all its weirdness, I was okay with her staring at me, because she was pretty.

When we finished our breakfast, Zion handed me a pair of boots. I put them on, laced them up, and followed him out of the tent to join the other miners. The men took off their shirts and took their tools in their arm. Then they headed for the mouth of the mine.

Several guards stood watch at the mouth of the mine while the others were on patrol. I sensed, from their casual interaction and banter between themselves, that the guards were relaxed, and not too observant of our movement. I guess it is human tendency to let your guard down a little when you fall into a routine, and not expect to encounter anything different.

We were about two hundred yards away, at the edge of the camp, huddled around thirty mining carts. Here, the multiple tracks merged into one and disappeared into the depths of the dark hole. One track branched off before it reached the mine, it headed to the left between the hill and the camp, disappearing into the woods.

"Come, get in the cart," said Zion.

Several men shielded me from the guard's sight as I slipped into the nearest cart. They pulled a canvas cloth over my body, stacked several sledgehammers and pickaxes on top, then wheeled me towards the mine.

We entered the mine without a hitch, just as Zion had planned the night before.

"Exiting the mine will be the challenge," Zion said to me in the cart. "The guards search the carts for the artifact."

I hoped that they would be as lackadaisical as they were when we entered.

Several hundred yards in, I pulled off the cover and popped my head over the edge of the cart. The air in the mine was stale, and the temperature had dropped. I didn't know how the men could come in here without shirts on. We went deeper into the mountain. Every hundred yards or so, we passed sconces on the wall holding torches that lit the tunnel and illuminated the gray rock walls as we descended into the depths of the mine.

When we came to the end of the track, I hopped out of the cart and followed Zion onto a basket that was lowered down a shaft by several large ropes and a pulley overhead. Slowly we descended into the deepest finger of the mine.

I couldn't tell you how glad I was to reach the bottom and stand firmly on the ground again. We made our way through a mineshaft that branched off in all directions. When we came to the end, we entered a small, manmade cavern that was about thirty yards in diameter. Zion and the twenty others that were lowered down with me placed their torches into the sconces on the wall and surrounded the mound in the middle of the room.

"There it is," said Zion, his booming voice echoing throughout the mine.

The rock mound in the center of the room was three feet high and had chisel marks all around it. It was noticeably darker than the rock walls that surrounded us but had a certain magical sheen to it.

Zion spoke while I stared at the mound, "After fifty years of working this mine, Panther had become a distant memory and I was beginning to doubt the legend. Then, about a year ago, I found something strange in this lower shaft. I was returning from a break when the wall caught my attention. I realized that the pattern in the rock made the shape of a panther. I looked at it multiple times, wondering if my eyes were deceiving me or if it was truly there. My fellow miners saw it, and knowing the legend from my story, they believed in it as a sign. It took us several months to dig out this chamber."

"What is it?"

"We don't know," Zion said, circling around the back of the chamber. "It is a type of rock we have never seen before.

"It is metallic-like and it's super hard," said a miner next to Zion.

"Every one of us has tried to break it, but it does not give."

"Like it is protecting something," said another miner.

"The artifact," I said.

I thought for a moment. "STRENGTH" kept popping into my head.

"Who is the strongest here?" I asked.

"I am," replied Zion. "I've already tried a thousand times to break this."

"Each one of us has tried," said another miner.

"Yeah, we all have," replied Zion.

The room went silent as Zion's words bounced through my thoughts.

We all have.

I stared at the twenty men huddled around. It hit me like a hammer—STRENGTH!

"There is someone stronger than you who can break this!" I said enthusiastically.

I looked at the confusion on Zion's and the other miner's faces.

"Who?" Zion asked.

"Why, *all* of you," I said nonchalantly.

"The engraving on my tablet said, *There is strength in one, and one strength in all.* One of you alone can't break this, but how about all of you at once?"

The mood in the chamber grew thick, and the power and energy magnified as the men steadied themselves and readied their hammers. I stepped back out of the way and stood at the mouth of the chamber to watch.

"Now, all at once—on three!" Zion commanded.

"One."

They hefted their hammers.

"Two."

They steadied their hammers behind them.

"Three!"

Each miner swung the fat metal head of his hammer in an arch overhead and hit the mound with great strength, precision, and synchronicity. My hands shot to my ears. With the loudest bang I have ever heard in my life, I thought I was deaf. They struck repeatedly at the rock, and each time, the power bounded off the mound and reverberated through the mineshaft.

On the fifth hit, a small crack formed in the center. The men began to chant as they swung.

"An ounce of strength—is the strength of a POUND!"

They wound up and struck the mound when they said "pound." With every hit they chanted louder, their blows gaining strength with their voices. I counted fifty hits before the dark gray substance finally crumbled.

Having triumphed over the rock, the men halted. They set their hammers on the ground and stared in awe. My ears rang something fierce as I stepped forward and peeked between two of the miners. I already knew what was in the middle of the mound amongst the broken pieces, but I had to see myself to believe it.

My eyes beheld the largest, most brilliant diamond ever. It was the size of an apple, and it shimmered in the torchlight, showing its magnificence. I was not sure if this was really happening or if this was a dream.

Zion and the others looked at me with satisfaction. "The artifact is yours."

I looked around the chamber at everyone, not sure what to do. I imagined that one of them might want to give the artifact to the Prime Ministerial himself. Then, I remembered the Fetcher's creed and realized that the Brotherhood of Fetchers was much stronger than any such impulse like that.

"Go ahead, take it boy," said the miner standing

next to me. He gave me a little nudge.

I stepped onto the pile of rubble and carefully took the jewel in the palms of my hands. I lifted it into the air for all to behold. It reflected a thousand prisms onto the walls of the cave. Inside the dazzling diamond were the roots and branches of the white tree.

"Go in STRENGTH!" I said and placed it into the other pocket of my satchel.

"Now, we must get you out of here," Zion said worriedly.

The miners left the chamber praising and patting each other on the back for a job well done. With a newfound spring in their step, they met up with a hundred or so other miners to spread the word and continue their daily work. We had to finish a full day's work so that the guards would not think something was up by us coming out of the mine early.

Zion and I stayed in the chamber and ate a bit of dried meat.

"I knew you would have the answer," he said between bites of jerky. "It was so simple, but we never thought of hitting it as one group."

"It was the tablet," I said humbly.

"But you thought of it," Zion said, then changed the subject. "You know you have a long road ahead of you."

"I know."

"I will help you as long as I can."

"Thanks," I said.

Zion nodded and we said nothing more until it was time to leave.

HUNTED

The pounding of my heart filled the inside of the cart. The chatter from wheels and the footsteps of the miners bounced off the walls of the mineshaft. I tried to control my breathing and relax, but it didn't work. I had the second artifact in my satchel, and I was too anxious about being discovered.

When the sun bore through several small holes in the canvas that covered me, I knew we had exited the mouth of the mine. I heard the muffled sounds of the guards as they stopped our progress to inspect the rubble.

After a moment of tense waiting, a guard rammed a pole between the tools in my cart. Luckily, he missed my legs, and hit the metal bottom with a loud crack. Looking up through one of the small holes, I watched the guard turn and wave Zion and the others on. The guards had been complacent. The artifact was right under their noses, and they didn't even know it.

I was relieved when we were on the move again. I knew that if we made it back to the end of the rail line I would be in the clear. I could make it back into the woods, find Wasgo and figure out our next move.

When the carts stopped, Zion pulled the heavy tools off my body and threw off the canvas. The sunlight that beamed through the surrounding trees blinded me for a moment as I stood up in the cart and got the blood flowing to my legs so they would work.

Zion steadied me as I climbed out of the cart. I held on to the satchel, so the tablet didn't smash against the metal sides. I was glad to have both feet planted firmly on the ground.

My satisfaction, however, was cut short. Instantly we were surrounded by fifteen guards on horseback. Those who had hammers in their belts grabbed them and prepared for a fight.

"I wouldn't do that if I were you," said a familiar voice from the edge of the trees.

I looked past the horseman and saw the Prime Ministerial.

"We have your women and children," he said pointing into the trees where thirty of his guards held onto the miners' family members. "I am sure you wouldn't want anything to *happen* to them."

I watched several of the miners lower their hammers. I looked into Alisa's scared eyes as a guard clasped a hand down on her shoulder.

"I know the boy has the artifacts, now hand him over," the Prime Ministerial commanded. "If you do without incident, you will not be punished before being dispatched to your next assignment."

Zion and a few of the larger men tensed up.

I knew what was going to happen before it did.

"An ounce of strength—is the strength of POUND!" Zion shouted.

Wasgo darted from the forest and attacked. He went for the back of a guard that was holding Alisa, and caused the others guards to turn from their prisoners in defense. In that split second of uncertainty, the miners threw their hammers with precision, knocking half of the guards off their horses.

One horseman spurred his horse straight at me. Zion grabbed a sledgehammer out of the cart, swung it around, and hit the guard in the upper thigh, breaking his femur. The guard dropped his reins and fell from the horse. Frozen in place, all I could do was watch him scream in agony as he writhed before me.

"Go with STRENGTH!" Zion shouted to me. He launched the sledgehammer in the air, missing the Prime Ministerial's head by an inch.

The women and children screamed as they escaped the clutches of their captors, and the miners, guardsmen and horses rushed at each other in a struggle for supremacy. I turned my pity away from the broken guard in front of me and found the courage to run. I went straight through the carnage, untouched and found Alisa rooted to the ground. I grabbed her hand and pulled her into the forest with me. We ran as fast as possible, considering I was pulling her against her will.

With the sound of hammers and metal clashing behind us, I picked our way through the trees and the underbrush. I felt Wasgo behind me as we separated ourselves from the camp and mine.

When we reached a small clearing, Alisa tripped on a branch and fell flat on her face. I turned back to help her to her feet and realized we were not alone. A guardsman on horseback emerged from the trees and circled us.

"Now, I have you!" he said, holding his sword out to Alisa's throat. "Don't run, and I will spare your lives."

Wasgo jumped between the guard and us, snarling at the horse. The horse reared and kicked his hooves at Wasgo. Wasgo took a hoof to the head and fell limp to the ground. My eyes flew to Wasgo as he lay there on the wild grass and hemlock of the forest, unmoving.

As a second guard stepped from the trees, I knew we were trapped; and there was nothing we could do but surrender. Surely, they would catch us if we ran.

Out of the corner of my eye, I saw a black blur streak from the trees to my right. In two giant leaps, a mass of fur bounded across the clearing and tackled the horse, knocking both guards, like dominoes, to the ground.

Alisa screamed as Panther sprang to its feet, circled the horse, and attacked the guardsmen.

Grabbing her hand, I yanked her arm, and dragged her through the trees again to escape. Looking past her long black curls, I noticed Panther was gone, relieved that he was not following us. I spied Wasgo's fur among the bodies and thanked him for his sacrifice for us.

After a while, we stopped running and caught our breath. There was a rustling in the bushes—coming towards us—and I picked up a rock. I wondered if it was Panther or another guard coming after us. As the figure emerged around a tree trunk, I threw the rock and hit the figure.

"Now, why would you do a thing like that?" Zion questioned, rubbing his chest.

"Papa!" Alisa said and ran to his open arms.

Zion gave her a big, comforting bear hug. "My darling, I am glad you are safe."

"Panther saved us," she said.

"I know," he replied. "It showed up in camp as the fighting began."

"And your wolf?" Zion asked.

"Dead . . ."

"I'm sorry to hear that," Zion said, pausing for a moment. He understood my loss. "We must move. More guards have arrived, and they are searching for you. If I can track you, they can. I know of an old mine rail near here that will take us to the coast."

We followed Zion until the trees parted at a pathway at the base of two hills. We followed that until we came to a large metal shed.

"The rail should be on the other side of this shed," Zion said. "First we need to get a cart."

Zion slid the hammer out from the holster on his belt and smashed the lock open. We entered the dark shed.

"Get in the last cart over there."

I helped Alisa climb in, hopped over the metal side, and sat down next to her. Zion threw open the shed doors, letting a flood of light into the shed. Down a slight decline ran a long thin rail line, disappearing into the distance.

Zion appeared behind us, uncoupled the cart, and pushed us outside.

"Ready for a wild ride?" he said, his grin showing through his goatee.

A lump formed in my throat as I remembered what Zion had said last night. I knew this line was headed downhill to the coast.

Just as he was about to push us off, I heard a howl from the forest behind the shed.

"Wait!"

"What is it?" Alisa asked.

"It's Wasgo.

The howl got closer.

"He's coming. We must wait for him."

"What if it is a warning? We must go!" Zion said, his words tinged with urgency.

"Wait a minute, Papa," Alisa said calmly.

Zion's muscles, already tense, readied themselves to push the instant the minute was up.

A furry beast rushed around the corner of the shed and leaped into the cart. I hugged Wasgo as he licked Alisa and me enthusiastically in the face.

"Hold on tight!" Zion said.

A HAIRY RIDE

The ride was fast but short.

Zion released the brake handle, pushed with all his might and the cart lurched forward down the rusty line. As it gained speed, Zion jumped into the cart and sat behind us with his hands firmly gripping the edge of the cart.

We cruised along at a safe speed—until we reached the drop-off. I thought my teeth were going to shatter as they clattered together on our ride down the uneven rails. I was glad I had put my satchel on my right, to the inside of the cart, or the tablet would have smashed against the metal side as the cart jostled back and forth—my ribs took the beating instead.

"Hold on tight," Zion said, pulling the break to control our speed.

"We are coming to a curve!" Alisa shouted.

"Get ready to jump and roll," Zion replied. "We are going a bit too fast. I don't know if I can slow the cart down enough to make the turn."

Zion braced his feet against the sides and pushed the hand brake back as hard as he could. The metal shoes of the brake bit into the wheels and shot sparks three feet out behind us. I wanted to put my hands over my ears to muffle the sound of screeching metal, but I knew I had to hold on and ready myself in case we needed to roll.

We hit the turn at a rather fast clip. The inside wheels came off the track, so Alisa and I threw our weight to that side. The wheels slammed back down onto the rails, and we continued around the bend.

"That was close," I said, looking over Zion's shoulder at the curve melting into the distance.

"That is not the worst of our problems," Zion informed us, pointing ahead.

I turned my head and stared at the steep run leading to a ravine that intersected the tracks.

"The bridge is out!" I shouted over the clanking wheels.

"We have to jump," Zion shouted back.

I looked at him sideways. "We're going way too fast to jump—we'll break our necks."

"It's either that, or we go over the edge and fall into the ravine."

"Well, if you put it that way—we'll jump."

The cart sped up as we raced towards the ravine. Zion pushed on the brakes. It barely slowed us down. The trees were passing by so fast, the trunks and branches blurred into one brown and green mass. We had about three thousand feet before we reached the broken rails that hung out over the craggy precipice.

With a loud crack as the brake handle broke free. Zion was thrown off balance. Thinking fast, I grabbed his leg and hung on with all my might.

"Thanks," Zion said, righting himself. "I thought I was a goner."

"What are we going to do now?" Alisa asked. "We don't have any brakes."

With little time to spare, Zion took his hammer out and wedged the metal head between the carriage and the rear wheel. He pushed against the brake mechanism. The hammerhead rubbed against the wheel and sparks flew in all directions. Several landed on the bare skin of his forearm, but he gritted his teeth and held the hammer tight.

"We are slowing down. Jump! Now!" Zion shouted.

Alisa jumped first. I watched her roll down the gravel embankment and get up shakily. Wasgo leaped out of the cart and landed dexterously on all fours. I jumped, twisted my ankle and fell hard onto my shoulder. I rolled down the embankment like a log and came to a stop when my back hit the base of a tree.

Dizzy, I sat up and watched the sparks move down the tracks. Zion continued to break the cart, but the end of the tracks came too quickly for him—he and the metal box flew over the edge and into the ravine.

GOOD FORTUNE

Alisa screamed. She took off like a gazelle, running along the tracks, and skidded to a stop at the edge of the cliff, shouting something back at me.

As my dizziness lessened, I finally understood what she was saying.

"He's alive. He's hanging from a beam. Come help!"

I stood up and ran to the edge to see her father hanging from a support beam of the broken bridge.

"Are you all, right?" I asked him.

"Yes," he replied. "I'm just hanging out and enjoying the view!"

Zion used his muscular upper body to pull himself onto the beam. I held onto a rail and grabbed one of his hands to help pull him back onto the safety of the cliff.

"Thanks," he said.

"No problem," I replied.

"You scared me," Alisa said rushing up to him. She threw her arms around him and sobbed into his chest. "I thought you were dead."

"It's all right pumpkin," he said, while caressing her head.

"How did you do it?" I asked.

"Luckily, I saw the beam and launched myself from the cart at the right moment."

"We've had a bit of good fortune today—haven't we?"

"Yes," Zion replied. "Yes, we have. Although, we are not that far from camp, and we have quite a way to go to reach Port Valec. We are going to need some more fortune to make it there without being captured."

Alisa and I nodded in agreement. We would need some more good fortune. In that moment, I realized that I had had nothing but good fortune these past few days. I was beginning to wonder if it would run out—*when* it would run out. It was only a matter of time, really.

I glanced down and noticed the burns on Zion's forearm. I reached into my satchel, took out the extra shirt I had, ripped off a strip of fabric, and handed it to him.

"We have to keep moving," he said, as he wrapped it around his forearm.

I turned to Wasgo, who was now beside me. "You know these forests," I said to him. "How do we get across this ravine?"

Wasgo barked and headed into the forest on our left.

Alisa looked at me with a quizzically.

"He led me to your camp."

"That wolf is smart." Alisa said.

"Yes, he is." I said. *If you only knew,* I thought.

We followed him into the forest along the jagged cliff of the ravine. Zion and Alisa held hands behind me as we picked our way down the steep incline to the base of the hill. A little while later, Wasgo picked up a game trail and we headed west along it. The trail ran along the edge of a stream, which gave us respite from the sharp hawthorn branches that scratched at our arms and legs as we passed quickly through the trees.

Keeping a steady pace, we followed the trail for

much of the early afternoon. We crossed the stream and turned north along the edge of the forest until the trees thinned out and stopped abruptly at the edge of a cornfield.

I looked back at the way we had come. I thought I heard the sound of hooves nearby and waited for a Guard to appear through the forest at any moment—but it didn't.

"What do we do now?" I asked Zion.

"Your guess is as good as mine," he replied, "We are leaving the forest. I guess we must move towards town and hope we aren't seen out in the open."

I felt the loss of the security of the forest as we left it and began trudging through the rows of corn. After a half hour, my calves burned from the laborious clumping through the soft ground at the base of the stalks and I twisted my ankle again, on chunk of dirt.

"I have to stop," I said, and rubbed my ankle.

"You wait here a moment. I think I see a building up ahead. I am going to go check it out."

Zion left Alisa, Wasgo, and me to rest while he went on ahead. I sat on the mound of dirt that the row of corn was planted in and massaged out my throbbing ankle.

"Does it hurt bad?" she asked.

"A little. I think it will be all right though—I am more tired of walking than anything."

"Yeah, me too," She replied.

Just then, Zion appeared.

"There is a farmhouse up ahead. I don't think anyone is home," he said excitedly. "Rest time is over— we need to keep moving."

Zion gave me a hand and I stood up, testing the strength of my ankle. There was a slight sting up my leg, but nothing I couldn't handle. Besides, I knew we had to keep going or the guards would catch up to us.

We followed Zion to the end of the cornfield and snuck around to the back of the farmhouse.

"What are we doing?"

"I saw some bread cooling on the window ledge," he said. "You two grab some clothes off the line and change out of those fetcher shirts—I'll meet you there in a minute."

Alisa and I walked over to the clothesline and eyed the fresh garments that swung gently in the breeze.

"Isn't this stealing?" I asked her.

"Yes, it is," came a gruff voice behind me.

I spun around and came face to face with the barrel of a musket, held by its owner.

"What are you two doing here?" The portly man looked down at the Fs on our shirt. "Why are you Fetchers trying to steal my clothes and bread?"

Just then, Zion rounded the corner, cradling a large loaf of bread in one arm.

The man turned his gun on Zion.

"Stop right there or you're a dead man!"

Zion stopped in his tracks. "Wait a minute mister, we don't want any trouble."

"Trouble," he said, and flicked the gun towards Zion's armload of food. "You just stole my bread, and these two here were about to steal my wife and kid's clothes."

"It's not stealing if I buy it from ya."

Zion carefully pulled a small pouch out of his trouser pocket and placed a small diamond down on the log that sat beside the clothesline pole.

"And if the Ministerial Guard comes looking . . ." Zion deliberately placed another diamond on the log. "You'll tell them we went the other direction."

The man nodded, lowered his gun, picked up the two diamonds. "I don't care for the Ministerial. So, whatever you've done be off with ya."

"Can I buy a horse from you?" asked Zion.

"No. I need em," replied the farmer.

Zion displays a large ruby. "How 'bout a ride to town then?"

"I was jist about to head there," said the farmer, with a huge grin.

The farmer swiped at the ruby, but Zion held it out of his reach.

"You can have it when we get to town, safely," said Zion. He put the ruby back in his pouch.

"I've got a cart of hay in the barn," said the farmer, pointing the shotgun towards the dilapidated wooden structure next to the farmhouse. "You can hide amongst the hay on our way to town." The farmer turns and heads into the barn.

Fletcher looks to Wasgo. "Should we trust him?

Wasgo moved his head up and down.

They followed the farmer into the barn.

PORT VALEC

They quickly changed into the new clothes while the farmer prepared the team of horses and hitched them to the cart. A young boy brought a pot of stew along with some spoons and bowls and set it down near Fletcher and the others.

"Mama made some stew for y'all," he said, handing out the utensils. "When you are done my Pa will take you into town."

"Thank you . . . Er . . ."

"Rowan."

"Thanks Rowan, your family didn't have to do this."

"The Ministerial could hang you for treason," Alisa chimed in.

"We know," said Rowan. "The Ministerial is not well liked in these parts—it's the least we could do for *the one.*"

I looked at him quizzically.

Rowan read my look and sat down on the hay bale, "News travels fast. Only a few days ago, reports came from San Fargo that *the one* had found the first artifact. When we saw the F on your shirts when you came out of the cornfield, my Pa had a feeling. When the guards quizzed him, he stalled them long enough for me to catch up to you."

"We're much obliged," Zion said. He wiped the stew sauce from his chin with the back of his hand.

We continued eating while Rowan told us about his farm. The stew warmed my belly and fueled my soul. His mother's home cooking was a hundred times better than the mush that the cooks at San Fargo made and called stew.

When we finished eating, I grabbed my satchel and pulled out the map and the tablet. I laid them out carefully on the bale in front of me.

"Not only was the first artifact found . . . but the second one as well," I whispered to Rowan.

I saw his eyes light up with excitement.

"We must get down the coast past San Fargo to Mount Norchet. I believe the third article is in the volcano."

"What makes you say that?" Rowan asked.

"Well, as the legend says, the first article was hidden in the waters. I found the first one diving in the seas around San Fargo. The second article was hidden in the ground. Zion here is from the mines of Etonia, where we found the second article. The third article was hidden in fire—where else is there fire but in a volcano?"

"Good thinking," Alisa said.

"A ship is leaving port in the morn'n," Rowan interrupted. "'Tis heading for Gullet—which takes you right past Mt. Norchet."

I looked at Zion. *Coincidence? Good Fortune? Or Dumb luck?* I thought.

"We have a cart of grain an' hay we must load on the ship tonight."

"Sounds like a plan," Zion said.

I re-packed my satchel tightly, so as not to lose anything, and followed Rowan and the others out of the loft. We hid in the cart between the grain and the twined bales of hay. Rowan's father placed several bales across the top concealing us from prying eyes and we headed down the road to Port Valec.

For the entire ride, I was worried that the Ministerial guards would check the cart and find us hidden beneath the hay. We had been in the cart a while when I heard the cart's wheels cross a wooden bridge, then the distinctive metallic clatter of horseshoes on cobblestone.

"I always like riding through the town center," Rowan said to his father.

"Yes, it is a sight to see as you cross through to the port," he replied.

I looked out of the crack between the hay bales and watched the black trimmed whitewash walls of the city pass by. The buildings were much different than those of San Fargo.

I must come back here one day. I thought to myself.

The cart finally stopped at the wharf. I peered through another crack as Rowan's dad talked with someone associated with the ship. They shook hands and the stranger disappeared up the gangplank and into the massive ship.

"We got you passage on the ship," Rowan said lifting a bale from off the top of our hiding place. The salty sea air rushed in to replace the dry smell of hay and hit me with a wave of nostalgia. I didn't realize then just how much I missed the sea air—but I didn't miss San Fargo one bit.

"Quickly, take a sack of gain up into the ship— before someone sees you," Rowan said urgently. "The Captain said you can stow below until he shoves off."

I hopped off the cart and hefted a huge sack of grain over my shoulder. Wasgo jumped over the rail and bounded ahead of us onto the deck of the ship. I struggled up the gangplank, almost falling off several times. Alisa, carrying her own stack of grain, traipsed up the brow with ease and agility. I hadn't realized how strong she was—it must have been from helping around the mine. Either that or I was just a weakling.

We hauled our supplies across the deck. I looked over my shoulder at the cart and didn't see Rowan's father anywhere. He had not followed us up to the ship. I looked around at the buildings and saw five figures standing in the shadow of one of the corner shops. The distinct silhouette of Ministerial Guard uniforms stood before Rowan's father, talking. I watched his father motion out and around with his hand and I could tell he was explaining to them that we were on our way to Gullet.

I was confused. Why would he do this after he had helped us? Why not just give us up at the farmhouse?

It was a moot point now. We were on the ship with nowhere to run. Soon Rowan and his father would be back, safe at their farm while the ship was stormed by the Ministerial Guard, and we were captured.

I sat with fists clenched and my stomach in knots.

How could I be so stupid as to fall for this? I thought.

Finally, after hours of worry, I succumbed to sleep.

SEA BREEZE

I woke disoriented. It took me a moment before I realized we were still on the ship. The sounds above us told me that dawn had come, and the crewmembers had set the ship loose from the wharf; we were drifting out to sea. Last night, the Ministerial Guards never appeared. I didn't understand why they hadn't captured us if they knew where we were. Maybe it was all part of Goah's plan. I had found the first two artifacts, maybe I was supposed to find the others too.

I leaned back, rested my arms on the satchel. I was startled out of my musings when several deckhands appeared and pointed the tips of their swords at us.

The captain appeared out of the shadows and stood before us.

"What's this all about?" Zion asked.

"It's been told to me, by the farmer, I am to transport you to Gullet and hand you over to the Prime Ministerial—you, and this beast, are now prisoners."

Traitor. I thought. *I knew it was too easy getting on this ship.*

I felt Wasgo's body tense as he readied himself to launch an attack on the captain. I quickly grabbed the fur on the back of his neck.

"Not now Wasgo," I said to him softly. I felt him

relax under my grip.

"Lock them up in brig until we reach Gullet," commanded the Captain.

The deckhands picked us up and shoved us into the metal cage. As the steel bars of the cage clanged shut and the lock was fit, I wondered if we were going to get out of this one.

"We'll figure a way out of this," Zion said, reading—correctly—the expression of anger and uncertainty on my face.

"We've been lucky to this point," I replied. "Hopefully something will happen to get us out of this jam."

I sat down in the corner, pulled my legs to my chest, and rested my chin on my knees. I had to think. I needed a plan of some kind.

Around mid-day, a stout man brought us a plate of bread and cheese. He set a jug of wine and some metal mugs near the door.

"Better eat up," the man grunted. "'Tis the only food you'll get before we reach Gullett. We're passing San Fargo now an' we'll be at Gullett before this afternoon."

Zion pulled the tray, jug and cups into the jail cell through the bars, and we ate our meager meal. Again, my thoughts turned to San Fargo. I missed my bell tower, feeling the cool breeze of the sea drifting over the rooftop and touching the skin on my face.

I tossed Wasgo a chunk of the stale bread. He snatched it out of the air and gulped it down in one move, then turned around, laid his head on the floor and closed his eyes.

I knew I should relax too, but all I could do was anticipate our imminent capture. The thoughts in my head were more torture than being locked up in the keel of this ship. In the middle of my disillusionment, the seeds of escape began to sprout and work their roots around in my head.

LIFEBOAT

When I felt the ship change directions and heard the bustling of the sailors above, I realized we must be getting close to Gullett. I knew I had to do something to get us onto the deck of the ship. We needed to commandeer a lifeboat and escape. I whispered my plan to Wasgo.

"Alisa," I said waking her from her nap.

"What?" she asked, rubbing her eyes.

"We need to get the guard to come, so we can get on deck."

"Why?"

"We don't have a chance of escape if we are still sitting here locked up when we come into port. Here, take this." I handed her an empty metal mug.

"A mug . . . what's this for?"

I didn't have time for a full explanation. "I have an idea, but I don't know if it is going to work—let's just get on deck."

From the way Alisa looked at me, I knew she didn't think that was a good enough explanation.

I picked up my metal mug and started clanking it against the bars. Alisa followed suit.

After a minute, a guard approached the brig. "That racket is killing my ears," the man said.

"We request to see the captain," I said.

"He's busy. He doo'nt want to see ya."

The man chortled and started to turn away. I quickly clunked my mug against the bars again. The guard spun around.

"He may want to see this," I said, holding the diamond up in my hand.

The guard stopped, mesmerized. Even in the dim light, the diamond shone dazzlingly, catching his attention.

"Oh, he'll be want'n to see that," the man agreed, and returned to unlock the cell. "You can give me that!" he said, reaching for the diamond.

Zion grabbed the guard's wrist and clamped his hand down tight, ready to break it.

I tucked the diamond back into my pack.

"Take us to the Captain," Zion said before hr released the man's wrist.

"Right away."

The guard led us out of the cell. He was rubbing his wrist as he took us topside. The instant we appeared on deck the other crewmembers swarmed us, thinking we had escaped. I thought my arms were going to break as the crewman who grabbed me yanked them behind my back and jerked them upward.

"Wait!" shouted the guard who let us out.

He reached for my satchel, ready to take the diamond from me. Wasgo growled and snapped at this hand. The guard jerked it away just in time to avoid the snapping jaws.

"They have something to show the captain," he said, counting his fingers, making sure they were still there.

The others looked at him hesitantly.

"Trust me, he will want to see it."

The men loosened their grips, but they none-the-less held on as they escorted us to his cabin door where the first mate knocked long and hard.

"What is it?" boomed the angry voice behind the door.

"Cap'n—we have som'pin to show you."

A moment later, I heard footsteps behind the door, the latch clicked, and the wooden door flung open. I noticed the captain was startled to see us standing before him with his crew. Composing himself, he grabbed his tricorn hat from the hook on the wall and took a moment to smooth his greasy black hair with his hand before donning his hat. Thus prepared, he stepped from the room.

"What is this about?" he commanded. "Who let these prisoners out of the brig?"

"I did sir," said the guard.

"And what did ya do that fer?"

"The boy here has som'pin to show you."

"Oh, does he?" he questioned, eyebrows raising. "What is it boy—yer wolf turns into a kitten?"

The crew sniggered at his meager attempt at a joke.

"Let the boy go, so he can show the cap'n what he has."

The man holding me let go of my arms. I shook the numbness out as the blood pumped back into my limbs. I pulled my satchel around and was about to take the diamond out when Wasgo intervened.

He stood up on his rear haunches and morphed into a man in front of us all.

The first mate and several other crewmembers dropped to their knees in fright. Others dropped their swords on the ground and ran for cover. All let go of their captives, and while some crossed their fingers and held them against their chests to ward off evil, most just stood there with their mouths agape—utterly speechless.

The captain was one of the latter.

Wasgo spoke, "You will let us go, or I will tear this ship apart with my powers."

That was all he had to say. They were terrified.

"We need your lifeboat," I said.

"Lower the lifeboat," the captain whispered.

Wasgo turned back into Wolf and walked undeterred to the lifeboat, where the first mate and five others were readying the boat for us. We hopped in, and they lowered us down to the water.

"Looks like our luck has returned," Alisa observed.

"Luck, and a lot of superstition!" I said.

We all laughed as Zion rowed us away from the ship towards the towering cliffs and Mount Norchet, which loomed behind them.

STAIRWAY TO HEAVEN

With every passing wave, the lifeboat surged towards the jagged rocks. Zion struggled to row us through the thrashing waves along the cliffs, without getting too close. After a half hour of constant rowing, I could tell he was tiring.

"I have to row . . . back out to sea," he said between strokes. "We can't climb . . . up these cliffs . . . and I haven't the strength . . . to keep wrestling . . . these waves."

Just then, something on the cliff caught the corner of my eye. Built into the rock I thought I saw a stairway.

"Over there." I pointed over her left shoulder. "There's a landing and a stairway."

Zion rowed like a lunatic to draw us closer to the landing, all without us smashing into the cliff. Waves crashed along the flat base and sea spray drifted over the boat. The landing was surrounded by sharp protruding rocks, and there was little margin for error if he was going to guide us safely into the opening. After a few minutes, we finally approached the landing.

"Alisa . . . when we get to the edge . . . grab the rope . . . jump to the ledge . . . and tie us off!"

Zion grunted as he struggled to maneuver the boat to the landing. With one last great heave, Zion let out an enormous groan, and the nose of the boat thudded against the landing. Alisa lightly sprang over the edge of the lifeboat to tie us off and climb out quickly."

"Got it!" Alisa said triumphantly. "All tied off."

I stepped past Zion, who was collapsed forward on his thighs, with his arms dangling limp to the bottom of the boat. Wasgo leapt over him and joined Alisa and I on the landing. We gave Zion a chance to catch his breath.

Wasgo, Alisa, and I stood at the bottom of the stairway. The sea smashed against the rocks and sent a fine mist over the bottom of the stairway. I placed my hand on the cool rock face, feeling the wet slimy surface. It was good to be standing on firm ground again. Then my eyes followed each step as it led to the top.

"How many steps do you think there are?" I asked Alisa.

"Maybe a thousand," she replied.

We both stared in silence, looking at the steep incline awaiting us.

Zion regained his strength and joined us.

"Feeling better dad?" Alisa asked.

"Yes," he said rubbing one of his biceps. "My arms still ache, but I feel much better."

"Thanks," I said to him.

Zion nodded and smiled. "My pleasure."

"Well," Alisa said, "after these stairs, I don't think your arms will be the only thing hurting anymore.'

We all laughed.

Zion untied the boat and gave it a shove with his boot. A wave took hold of it and crashed it against the rocks. I was glad we hadn't been in the boat when it did that.

"There's no going back now," Zion said.

"Unless you want to ride on a splinter." Alisa

replied.

We chuckled some more, then began our arduous climb to the top.

THE RESCUE

Alisa took the lead, counting out each stair.

"One . . . two . . . three . . ."

I was glad to be heading up the cliff towards the third artifact.

After climbing a few hundred stairs, we stopped for a rest. We watched the pieces of the lifeboat toss about in the foamy water created by the violent surf against the cliff face.

I found my mind wandering as we continued our monotonous climb. *Where would we have been if we hadn't found this stairway? Would we have crashed against the rocks and drowned? Would we have been caught by the Ministerial's frigate? Like Alisa said, this truly was a stairway to heaven.*

Every hundred stairs there was a small landing. We were about halfway up when Wasgo slipped past Alisa and went ahead of us.

The constant replay of each step wore on our feet and legs. I could feel the burning deep in my muscles. This was the most steps I had ever climbed in my life. I didn't want to see another stair again, but—we were only halfway to the top.

Keeping away from the edge, I drug my hand along the rock wall. My gaze drifted away from the stair in front of me, out to the horizon. It was such a brilliant sight from our vantage point; the deep blue waters speckled with whitecaps stretched far off into the horizon. The coastline behind us meshed into the deep blue sea and disappeared into the afternoon haze.

In front of us, I could make out the port in the distance where several ships were anchored, including the merchant ship we had escaped from. Gullet was a massive city a thousand times larger than San Fargo and stretched as far as the eye could see.

I figured someone would be sending a ship any minute now to recapture us, so I quickened my pace in a bid to reach the top sooner. In my haste, I placed my foot on the stip Alisa still claimed. My clunky boot clipped Alisa's foot as it trailed on the step behind her, and she went sprawling over the edge of the stairway.

"Aaaaahhhhh!" she screamed as she fell over the edge.

My heart leapt into my throat as I realized what I had done.

Zion pushed me into the wall and leaned over the edge as he reached for his falling girl. He caught her hand at the last second, saving her for the moment. Zion strained to hold on. I moved to his side to help, but his arms were still tired from the excessive rowing, his hand lost its grip. Alisa fell again.

"Aaaaahhhhh!" she screamed as she fell a second time.

"Noooooo!" Zion shouted. "Alisaaaaa!"

I closed my eyes. *I wish it was me, instead of her.*

I waited for the nightmare to end. I felt powerless. There was nothing I could do to save her. I wished I could go back in time and prevent the accident from happening. All was silent for a second.

"She's on the edge of the cliff," Zion said, looking

back at me.

"What?" I asked, opening my eyes.

"She landed on a small ledge."

I leaned over the edge near Zion and looked down. I saw her standing on a small ledge, barely big enough for her two feet, about twenty feet down. Her fingers clawed into a rock that protruded off the wall. I was relieved that she was all right, but still worried that she might fall off that ledge. I wondered how long she could hang on there.

"How are we going to get to her?" I asked Zion.

"I would lower you down and pull you both back up, but my arms are so tired, and my grip is so weak, I'd drop you both."

Thinking quickly, I whistled.

Twenty seconds later, Wasgo came bounding down the stairs.

"I need you to shift," I explained to Wasgo.

Wasgo tilted his head sideways and perked his ears.

"It's okay—Alisa fell over the edge, and I need you to lower me down so I can grab her and pull her up. Zion can't do it—his arms are too weakened from rowing."

Wasgo shifted before our eyes. He grabbed my ankles and lowered me over the edge. Zion held onto Wasgo's waist, ensuring that he didn't fall headfirst down the cliff side while he hoisted me down.

I stretched my arm out to Alisa.

"Grab onto my arm!"

"No," she said. Her panicked face looked up at me.

"Alisa," I said calmly.

I could see her eyes looking down along the cliff to the water below.

"Alisa, look up at me."

She turned her gaze towards mine.

"Now, grab onto my arm—Wasgo and your dad will lift us up!"

Alisa was still paralyzed with fear.

"You have to grab my arm now, or we will all fall!"

Reluctantly, Alisa grabbed my hand with one of hers, still holding onto the rock with the other. When I had a good grip on her, she wrapped her other hand around my wrist. Her eyes pleaded for me not to drop her.

"I've got her, now pull us up." I shouted to Wasgo.

A minute later, we were standing on the stairwell, our backs up against the wall and away from the threat. The silence was thick, and all motion was slowed as I caught my breath. I distinctly felt my blood flow out of my head, back to the rest of my body as Wasgo stood by my side, on all fours, panting.

Zion hugged his little girl and kissed the top of her head, then turned and faced me. His arm was still clutching Alisa close. He looked grateful and angry at the same time—if that was possible. I could tell he was grateful to me for his daughter's rescue, and at the same time, scornful that I had toppled her over in the first place.

"Let's get off these stairs," he said.

I agreed, not wanting to talk about what had happened. I took the lead and quickly headed for the top. Immediately, I began thinking about what it would have been like for Zion to lose his child. Then I thought of my parents. I wondered what it was like for them to lose me to the Fetchers. To be taken away at such a young age, never to be seen again. Most other parents' children got to learn their profession at home, or in the village or town where they lived. I knew how hard it had been for me, having to leave them. I wondered, now, how it had affected them. With each step, the questions fired in my head.

Where are they? What are they doing? Are they still alive? Did they have other children? Did they miss me? Do they miss me?

By the time I reached the top I was nearly in tears. Questions I had suppressed for over ten years that had re-surfaced on that climb. Wasgo seemed to sense something was bothering me; he came over and rubbed his side against my leg.

"Thanks, Wasgo," I said, smoothing the fur on his head. "The near miss with Alisa back there got me thinking about losing my parents."

"Me too," Wasgo whispered.

We stood in silence as we waited for Zion and Alisa to catch up to us. I stared up the path that led to the side of the volcano and wondered if I would ever see my parents again.

MOUNT NORCHET

After climbing all those stairs, we took a quick break to catch our breath and relax from the tension of the near-death experience. When I felt ready, I stood up and eyed Mount Norchet looming overhead. Wasgo stood up and padded over to me.

"Do we have to go inside that for the next artifact?"

Wasgo looked up at me with wide eyes, tongue out, panting.

"Yeah, stupid question."

I looked over to Zion and Alisa.

"Shall we?"

They followed Wasgo up the winding pathway. After about two hours of walking back and forth, we had come to the end at the boulder field at the base of the volcano.

"Great!" I said, turning back to the others. "The path has disappeared under a lava flow."

"Where do we go now, father?" Alisa asked, from where she rode piggyback on Zion.

"Give me a moment," Zion said, crouching down to slide Alisa off his back.

We all looked up at the steep cliffs of the volcano and tried to figure out what our next move was going to be.

Zion held his hand over the flow. After a minute, he

stood up and pressed his foot against the lava flow then kicked it. After determining it was fine, he hopped up and tested it against his weight. The charred exterior held.

"Looks like it's cool," he said jumping down. "It's risky, but we'll have to climb."

I looked at the steep bank of the lava flow. From where we were now, one wrong step would send us on a thousand feet slide, down the rough incline, with a fall right over the cliffs.

I turned to Wasgo. "You might have to shift into human form for this one buddy."

Wasgo shifted. It was all right for him to do that being that Zion and Alisa had already seen him shape shift on the ship.

"We'll let Wasgo lead the way, and I'll bring up the rear," Zion said.

I nodded at Zion. I realized that he didn't want a repeat of what had happened earlier. He wanted to be there to catch us in case anyone slipped. Especially Alisa. I didn't blame him.

We picked our way, carefully towards the outcropping to our left. After thirty minutes of climbing, we made it to our destination, a landing at the base of a tunnel in the side of the mountain.

We stood on the flow of lava that had come out of the mouth of the tunnel, which was over three times as tall as Zion.

Wasgo shifted back into wolf form.

"Impressive!" Zion said.

"Yeah, I like it when he shifts," I said.

"No. The tunnel," Zion replied. "It's chiseled out so perfectly round and smooth."

I felt the cold granite walls of the tunnel. "Wow,

you're right, it is smooth."

Wasgo silently moved past me and disappeared into the darkness in front of us.

"I guess we follow him," Alisa said.

We made our way slowly along the tunnel. My eyes adjusted to the dim light as best they could but there came a point where we were surrounded by pitch-blackness. I kept walking forward, having only the sound of Zion and Alisa's footsteps ahead to guide me. The tunnel brightened suddenly, and we found ourselves entering the center of the volcano.

I stood for a moment, mouth gaping, awed by the magnificence of the guts of Mount Norchet. The uneven walls of the volcano towered several thousand feet overhead, and a circular orb of periwinkle greeted me from beyond the mouth. A sliver of light shone through the blue opening, illuminating the far wall of the interior chamber.

"Now that's impressive," I said.

"Yeah, but *that's* interesting," Alisa countered, pointing. "What is that?"

My eyes followed her extended arm to a raised mound in the center of the volcano. On top of the mound was what appeared to be an elongated box with carvings of the tree of life on the side.

"That's it!" I said, and immediately started moving towards it.

"Hold on," Zion said, grabbing the back of my tunic, pulling me backwards.

"What?" I asked.

"Look around the edge of the volcano."

The charred remains of bones and bodies littered the edge of the volcano.

"Oh," I gasped.

I hadn't realized, until then, that the mound in the middle was an island, and that there was an active lava ring around it.

"Let's move around to the back side to higher ground," Zion said. "Then we can figure out how to get across the lava."

"Right," I said, stepping over a charred skull.

I picked my way around the edge of the lava ring as Wasgo, Zion, and Alisa followed. We finally made it to the higher ground, twenty feet or so above the lava. Behind us was an identical tunnel that, I hoped, led out the other side of the mountain.

It was clear that the ring of lava was active as I peered out to the center island. Cracks in the black surface showed the bright orange magma that loomed just under the cooling surface. One step on that and I would have been fried.

"Are you seeing what I am seeing?" Zion asked.

"Yeah, impending doom," I said.

"No," Zion replied. "Look to the left of the island."

I shifted my gaze to the left. "I don't see anything."

"Don't you see the difference in the lava?"

I studied the lava harder and shook my head. "No."

"It looks darker in that one area." Zion pointed.

"It's like a path to the island," Alisa said.

"Yeah, I see it now," I exclaimed. "Maybe it's a hardened bridge to the island."

We started down the embankment along the side of the cavernous walls to where we saw the darker area of lava.

"Who's going to try it first?" I asked.

We all looked at each other.

"Fur and fire don't mix well," said Wasgo immediately.

"I'm too heavy," Zion replied. "I'll crack it and probably fall through."

"I'm the lightest," said Alisa.

"Oh no, you're not going!" Zion exclaimed and gave his daughter a stern look.

"I'll go," I replied. "Anyway, I'm the one that is supposed to get the artifact."

"I *am* the lightest, I'm going!" Alisa said to her father, with a stern look.

"Fine, you both will go," said Zion. "You better not let her fall in Fletcher, if she does, you'd better go with her!" Zion patted him on the shoulder. "Wasgo and I will go up top, and I'll shout directions to keep you on the bridge."

We waited for them to reach the overlook spot on the higher ground.

"Ready?" Alisa asked, looking over her shoulder at me.

She had more courage than I did, myself. The word "COURAGE" bounced around my brain. Then I remembered the tablet.

"Hold on . . ." I said and took it out of my satchel to read.

The first two words were "BELIEF" and "STRENGTH" and I meditated on what the tablet said about them. The third word on the tablet was "COURAGE". I read the inscription to Alisa.

Moral strength in light of danger or pain,
And willingness to withstand threat of death,
To endure hardship is bravery so.
Block out that which is difficult to bear.
To oppose is opposition enough.
Confront it and go forward with COURAGE.

That made sense, it was going to take a lot of courage for us to cross the lava bridge.

"Right," Alisa said. "Let's do this."

A LESSON OF COURAGE

I was unsure about this lava-bridge thing. I mustered up enough courage to take that first step towards following Alisa across to the island.

"Keep going straight!" Zion shouted from his overlook.

Alisa gingerly placed her foot on the lava in front of her, tested the spot, then stepped forward. We did this for fifteen minutes or so, which felt to us like hours had gone by.

"We're doing well," I said to Alisa.

On her next step, I heard a cracking noise that echoed through the cavern.

"You need to go more to your right," Zion shouted.

Alisa stepped right and eased her way forward again. I felt the heat on either side me rising—that or it was my own body temperature increasing from the stress of the situation. Either way, I knew it was not a good thing.

"The bridge looks like it's getting narrower!" shouted Zion.

"What?" I shouted back.

"The dark area is shrinking," he confirmed.

"It's getting hotter down here," I replied. "I think the bridge is melting."

"Move to your left two steps—get a move on!"

Alisa and I stepped to our left.

"Okay, if you go straight ahead now, you will make it!"

I heard another cracking sound underneath my foot.

"We'd better hurry!"

"I'm going for it," Alisa said, and sprang from her spot.

As if she were playing a game of hopscotch, she took three bounding steps and made it to solid ground. I followed suit and in no time stood firmly on the granite island in the middle of the volcano. I must admit, it was an impressive sight looking straight up out of the center of the massive Mount Norchet.

"Okay, great job," I said giving her a hug. "Going back will be a bit trickier."

"Yeah."

"Let's find this artifact."

I turned and began climbing up the slight rise to the top of the island. A stone box about eight feet long and three feet wide sat before us. Each side had the tree of life etched on its surface.

"Well, the artifact must be under there." I guessed, examining the lid. I dug my fingers under the lip and pulled. After a few tries of straining my fingers, I felt the lid lift from its place set into on the four sides.

Alisa helped me slide the lid off to the side and we peered in.

"Ahhhh!" She shrieked.

"What is it?" Zion shouted, his voice deep with concern.

"It's a stone coffin," I replied. "There's a body in here."

I looked at the decayed body dressed in the remnants of a Ministerial Guard uniform. I peered at the head, with tendons, muscle, and strands of brown hair still attached. Odd, but I think it was smiling at us. I wondered if this is what had become of Lorucias Guifachs, or if this were just an ordinary Ministerial Guard.

"Okay, here goes," I said, frisking the body for any signs of an artifact.

I had no clue what we were looking for. I checked the pockets; nothing. I took the watch off its wrist and examined it; it was plain, with no markings on it whatsoever. I had expected it to have at least the tree of life etched on it, but it didn't.

"I don't think this is it," I said to Alisa, holding up the watch.

"Where could it be?"

"I don't know," I said. "I'll lift the body and you look underneath."

"You want me to do what?"

"Alisa, we don't have time for this. I'll lift the body and you look underneath."

She looked mortified, and a little green, as I tilted the body to the side. She held her breath, scrunched up her face, then quickly searched all around the bottom of the coffin with her hands.

"Nothing there," she said, shaking her hands beside her, trying to remove the memory of what they had done.

Just then, we heard a loud roar that echoed through the chamber.

I looked up to where Zion and Wasgo stood—a ten-foot Grizzly Bear was standing on its hind legs, towering behind them. Zion looked white as a ghost as he stood frozen in the face of such horror. Wasgo wasn't moving either. Bear didn't seem to care about them. It crashed onto its front paws, bounded down the embankment, and circled around the lava pit to the bridge.

Bear sniffed the air in our direction then paced back and forth several times.

"What's he doing?" Alisa asked.

"It looks like he's thinking about crossing."

"What?"

"It's the protector of this artifact," I said. "He wants over here."

Suddenly Bear turned and placed its front paws on the cooler area of lava that made up the bridge across to the island.

"He's coming!" Zion shouted.

"What do we do?" Alisa shouted back.

"I don't know . . . throw some rocks at it," Zion suggested.

"Won't that make it madder?"

"Right . . . don't throw rocks at it," Zion replied. "We'll try to catch its attention."

Zion began shouting at Bear, and Wasgo howled.

Bear looked at them, then sniffed in our direction, then looked back at them. It was clearly confused.

"Hurry, find the artifact," Alisa said.

"Right." I looked down at the body in the coffin. Whoever it was, he was still smiling up at me. Leaning forward, I examined the head. I noticed something peculiar. The mouth had been sewn together. I started picking at the twine that held the leathery lips together.

"What are you doing?" asked Alisa, clearly appalled.

"I think it's in the mouth," I said.

"What?"

"I think the artifact is in the mouth. It has been sewn shut."

"Oooh . . . yuck."

I quickly undid the stitching and pulled down on its

chin. After a few cracks, the chin moved freely open and I saw a bit of white, and a flash of silver. Reaching in, I grabbed a small handle and pulled.

"Got it!" I said, holding the artifact for Alisa to see.

It was a corkscrew with a bone handle. Etched onto the top part of the bone was the great tree.

"That must be it," she said.

"I've got it," I shouted to Zion.

"Great," he yelled back. "We'll lure Bear away."

I watched Zion pick up a rock and throw it at Bear. He hit it in the shoulder. Bear stood up and roared at him. I could tell it was mad, but it didn't chase after Zion. Bear just turned and sniffed at us again. Zion threw another rock but this time it missed. It landed on the crusted surface of the lava in front of Bear, which drew its attention back to us.

"That's not working," Alisa shouted.

Bear walked on its hind legs to the edge of the lava, put its front paws together and then threw its full weight down onto the lava. As its paws hit, I heard the crack echo through the chamber. Bear did it again. There was another crack. On the third hit, Bear was successful in breaking apart a portion of the bridge. Bear stepped back, sat down, and stared at us.

"That's not good," said Alisa.

In a matter of seconds, the lava field surged to life. I felt the temperature rise all around us, and the orange molten rock boiled through the crusty surface. The lava engulfed the bridge and re-absorbed it back into itself. There was no way across now.

"What are we going to do now?" Alisa cried. "We'll burn up before it cools again."

"I have an idea."

I stuffed the corkscrew in one of the many pockets

of my satchel. "Sorry," I said to the body, and dumped it out of the coffin. I carried it around to the side near Bear and heaved it into the air towards the sitting beast. The body landed on the surface of the lava only a few feet away from us. It caught fire and melted into the lava instantly. Bear continued to stare at us. It was as if it knew that we were going to die, and it was watching with pleasure.

"Get in!" I urged Alisa.

She jumped into the coffin.

"I hope this thing floats," I said.

There was a faint scent of burnt flesh and singed hair in the air as I put my shoulder into the side of the coffin and pushed with all my might. The stone base slid easily on the granite surface. I was glad it was a small coffin and not a massive sarcophagus, or we would have been in trouble. There was still a chance we might still be burnt to a crisp if my plan didn't work.

I lined the coffin up with the shore opposite Bear. Zion must have seen what I was doing, for he was already on the shoreline waiting for us, with Wasgo.

"Are you ready?" I asked Alisa.

She sat facing me, in the middle of the coffin, knees against her chest. She placed her hands flat against the inside of the coffin to brace herself, not wanting to get lava on them, and nodded.

"One . . . two . . . three!"

I pushed and ran behind the coffin as it slid down the slope towards the lava ring. As it hit the lava, it floated! I quickly jumped into the makeshift boat, landing square in the center, sitting in front of Alisa.

The coffin-boat rocked a bit but sped across the lava none-the-less. I felt the stone heating up below my rear. I hoped that it wouldn't melt through before we made it to safety.

After a few agonizingly slow seconds, the boat slowed near the edge. It was too far to jump, and judging by our speed, it wasn't going to make it any further. Making a split-second decision, I grabbed the corpse's arm that hadn't fallen out of the coffin earlier and used it as an oar. It did melt, but it lasted just long enough for me to push us within jumping distance to shore.

"Jump!" I shouted to Alisa.

She turned where she sat, stood up, rested her foot on the edge of the coffin and launched herself into Zion's waiting arms. I felt the stone beneath my feet getting hotter, and the coffin began to list.

It was now or never. I mustered all the courage inside me, ran the length of the coffin, pushed off the edge, and sailed across the lava.

I landed on my side, at Zion's feet; the force knocked the wind out of me. I was disoriented for a moment, but not enough to miss the loud roar of an angry bear from across the cavern.

Zion helped me to my feet as I tried to breathe in.

"Run to the tunnel at the overlook!"

Holding on to Zion, I somehow got my legs to work, and made it to the overlook.

Bear met us there.

It stood on its hind legs, the full height of it blocking the entrance to the tunnel. I was still a little disoriented, but I heard perfectly. Bear roared. Alisa shrieked. Wasgo howled. Then silence.

No longer fighting to get air back to my lungs, my vision cleared, and I stood up.

I couldn't believe my eyes. Wasgo was in human form . . . talking to Bear that was now sitting as docile as a cub.

"Bear is all right now," Wasgo said, turning to face me. "He now knows that you are the chosen one."

"Why didn't you do that before?" I asked him.

"Some things have to play out a certain way for a reason," he replied.

"Somehow, I knew you would say something like that."

"It's true," he replied. "If I had done that earlier, you might not have found the courage to get back across the lava the way you did."

"But the bridge—" I said.

"Was melting anyway."

Wasgo shifted back into wolf form.

TAKEN PRISONER

The lava ring rose and flowed out the lower tunnel towards the cliffs. We escaped out of the higher tunnel and emerged on the other side of the volcano. Farther down the mountain, at the tree line, I saw the gray tops of the Fetchers' tents amongst the evergreen. They looked exactly like the tent had met Alisa in, back at the mines.

"Do we dare go into camp?" I asked Zion.

"Let's try to sneak by," he said. "This is the only trail, and it leads directly to the camp. But, if we go across the boulder field, it will be slow going, and we will probably be seen anyway, what with a giant bear trailing us and all."

"I guess we take the path and try to sneak by camp then."

We began our descent from Mount Norchet. About an hour leter, we noticed a small party traveling towards us. Someone in the camp must have seen us and sent a scouting party to meet us. I counted fifteen in the party, all dressed in gray robes with a crimson F on the front. They were Fetchers.

Another thirty minutes of hiking down the mountain, and we met face to face with the party. We stopped to greet them.

"Hello," I said to the first robed man.

He passed, silently, not even noticing Bear next to us.

Each robbed figure moved silently by the hoods pulled over their heads, hiding their faces. I noticed that the center hooded figure was much shorter than the others, and instead of walking tall like them, this figure was hunched over, feet shuffling along the dirt. As the figure passed, I heard a quiet sob coming from under the hood.

"Where are you going?" I asked the next person in the line.

They kept moving, ignoring my questions, as the rest passed in silence too.

"What's going on?" I asked the last person in line.

The figure broke off from the others and stopped in front of me. "We are the ceremonial fire party." A deep voice resonated from within the hood. "The *one* is going to retrieve the artifact."

I knew he was talking about the small, sobbing figure.

"You mean, going to his death." I replied.

"What do you know?"

"I know you have to stop them."

"There's no stopping the fire ritual." The hooded figure turned and walked after the others.

"Fletcher, let's go," Zion said.

"I can't let them send that boy into the lava." I dug my hand into my pouch. "Wait. I have the artifact!"

The last Fetcher stopped and turned. He pulled the robe off his head revealing his baldness. Finally, the man noticed Bear, then spied the corkscrew I held up in my hand.

"Halt!" he shouted to the others and rushed back

down the hill towards us.

Zion stepped in front of me to block the man's advance.

"You must put that away immediately," he boomed, as the others surrounded us.

A rumbling growl arose from the belly of Bear.

"Whoa," the man said. "I am only trying to protect you."

"So is he," I replied.

"We need to get you to the camp," he said. "A Ministerial Dispatch is coming from Gullet. He is expected at any moment. For what, I was not sure."

"We can't trust them," Zion whispered in my ear.

"I know," I said, "but we don't really have a choice."

I looked at the group surrounding us. Every one of them had now taken their hoods off. I stared into the tear-stained face of the boy who had been going to his death in the volcano. He was no older than I was. His soft blue eyes looked at me with a kind gratitude for saving his life.

"Lead us to camp," I said to the man who seemed to be in charge.

We hurried along the path to the tents. When we reached camp, the other Fetchers were surprised to see us—not only because we had a giant bear with us, but because the ritual party had returned so quickly.

Just then, two Ministerial Guards rode in on horseback.

"What's the nature of this?" One guard demanded.

"I have them sir!" the deep voiced Fetcher said. "They are the ones the Prime Ministerial is looking—"

Before he got out his last word Bear stood up, let out a deep growl, swiped at the back of the Fetcher with his sharp claws. The one who had betrayed us went flying five feet in the air. I watched him land in an unnatural position near a tent.

The horses reared as Bear charged through the crowd.

"Run Fletcher!" Zion yelled.

I sprinted past the tents and headed into the trees; Wasgo was by my side. I heard the hooves of the Guard's horses behind us. It seemed to me that being chased down by guards was becoming a normal occurrence for us.

I heard Alsia's scream. I couldn't help myself—I stopped and looked back. One of the guardsmen held her on his horse, his sword drawn across her chest. Zion was standing in front of the horse, pleading for his daughter's life.

The other guard circled around behind, to where Wasgo and I stood. Wasgo straightened his tail, tensed his muscles and growled in preparation for an attack.

"No, Wasgo," I said calmly. "They'll kill Alisa."

Wasgo backed down. "I'll be with Bear, watching and waiting," he said, as he ran off into the forest.

"We'll go with you," I said to the guards. "Don't hurt the girl."

The guardsman ushered me over to Zion, then led us to the far tent. They took my satchel, forced us to sit on the ground around the tent pole, and bound our hands and feet with rope. When the light of the day waned, a lone figure slipped into the dark tent and started untying my hands.

"Flethcer Barnes," a boy said.

"Yes," I replied.

"Someone wants to speak with you."

"Who?" I asked looking into the boy's face. I instantly recognized him as the boy on the mountain.

"You will know when you see him."

Thoughts ran through my head.

The Oraculum?No, he said him not them. The Prime Ministerial? No, we had not heard the dispatch had arrived yet. Who then? You will have to see.

"Hurry, come with me."

"Not until you untie my friends and let them go."

"But . . ."

"No," I said sternly. "They want me, not them. They are not a part of this—let them go."

I helped the boy free Zion and Alisa's bindings.

"We can't leave you," Alisa said.

"Yes, you can."

"I promised to protect you," Zion replied.

"I'll be fine," I said confidently. "Wasgo and Bear will protect me."

"All right," Zion said.

The boy and I held up the back of the tent as Zion and Alisa slipped under, out of the camp, and into the cover of the trees and the evening sun.

"Take me to my summoner," I said to the boy.

He led me out of the tent.

AN OLD FRIEND

I did not see any signs of the guards from earlier as we walked through camp. He led me past the campfires, where the Fetchers were busy preparing their evening stew, to a tent on the far side of the camp. I felt Wasgo following me; and I felt a little more confident after seeing the hulking outline of Bear out of the corner of my eyes.

As we approached the tent, I realized it was the only tent that was all red instead of gray with a ruby red F painted on each side.

Who is he taking me to see?

The man stopped at the tent, held open the flap, and motioned with his hand for me to enter.

I stepped into the candlelit tent. As my eyes adjusted, someone emerged from the shadow at the rear of the tent.

"Marcus?" I said, not believing my eyes. "Marcus Dunn, is that you?"

"Hello, my friend."

"Hello, my old *friend*," I replied.

I was confused. He was dressed in Fetcher's clothes but was in the Ministerial Guard's tent. I wasn't sure if I should trust him or not.

"As fortune has it, we meet again," he said. "Have a

seat, and I'll tell you the story of how I came to be here."

"Thanks, I'll stand," I said. "I've been sitting a while now."

"After we parted in San Fargo—"

"You mean after you pushed me in the river."

"Ah, yes. 'Twas only a little nudge to get you going on your adventure," he said smiling under his beard. "Anyway, after the Prime Ministerial knew that you had found the first artifact he sent the remaining Fetchers here, and to the camp in the western mountains. I was sent to the west, but I knew I had to get here in time for your arrival."

"Another one of your dreams?"

"Well, sort of," he said, and took a drink out of a glass sitting on the table. "On the trip, I daydreamed of fire and lava and knew I had to get here. When we arrived at camp, I slipped out in the dark of the night and made my way here. I had only just arrived to see you coming down the mountain. After the guards caught you, I snuck into this tent and knocked them out. They are over there in the corner."

I saw the two guards tied up against each other, with a red bandana in each of their mouths; the bandanas tied in knots at the back of their heads.

"I figured you'd need help escaping, so I sent my new friend to get you. I also figured you'd need this," he said, holding up my satchel.

I was surprised. Marcus could have kept it for himself and given it to the Prime Ministerial. He would have been a hero.

"Everything is in it."

I took the satchel from him and opened the flap. The tablet, map, bottle, diamond, and corkscrew were all in its own place.

"You'd better get going," he said. "The Prime Ministerial will be here any moment. The boy will have a horse waiting for you in the forest."

"Where should I go?"

"Well, you already found an artifact in water, earth, and fire. That leaves only air."

"Air."

"What rides on the air?"

"Birds," I replied.

"Yes, birds," he said and took another drink. "Supposedly, giant eagles live in the Aligeiri Mountains to the west."

"Yes, they must be the protectors of the last artifact."

"That is where you must go. Look for the tallest mountain. That is Plata's Peak. The artifact is probably there."

"Do I need to ask?"

"Saw it in a dream," he grinned.

"What will I look for?"

"That I do not know—I only saw the peak."

"Great," I said. "Thanks, Marcus."

"You are welcome my boy," he said. "Oh, here is a map for you. It's a little crude, as I drew it as I was escaping, but I marked where the camp is located. You will want to stay away from there, unless you want to get captured again."

"No, I'd rather not."

Just then, I heard a commotion outside. The sound of horses, and wagon wheels on dirt and horses clopping approached the tent.

"Go!" Marcus urged me.

I poked my head out of the front of the tent. Fetchers scrambled every-which-way as the Ministerial

Detail pulled up with the Prime Ministerial carriage.

"Oh, and Fletcher," Marcus said behind me. "Don't be afraid of falling."

ON THE RUN AGAIN

I sprinted across the path outside the tent, and darted between the trees of the forest, putting as much distance between me and the Prime Ministerial as possible. I was glad I didn't hear any hooves behind me this time. The guards must have been too busy with the arrival of the Prime Ministerial to have noticed me slip out of the tent.

Wasgo appeared by my side as I ran.

"I thought you'd never come out of there," he said.

"Yeah, me too. Strangest thing though, my old friend Marcus, from San Fargo, was in there. He had knocked out the guards and gave me my satchel."

"Goah works in strange ways," Wasgo said.

"Yeah, I guess so." I said, dismissing any misgivings I may have had.

He took the lead and directed me to where the boy was waiting as planned with the horse.

"Here you go," said the boy.

Suddenly a large hand fell on my shoulder.

Turning, I stared into the distressed face of Zion. "What has happened, Zion?"

"Alisa and I got separated, and she was captured," he said, shaking his head. "The dispatch has Alisa."

"We have to get her back," I said firmly.

"No, a couple of guards left with her a while ago. I

166

heard them say they were taking her to Gullet.”

“We go to Gullet then,” I said, placing my hand on his arm in a futile attempt to comfort him.

“No, you go finish what you started.” He tapped my shoulder. “I’ll get her back and meet up with you later.”

“It will be okay,” I said, for myself as well as him. “Meet me in the center of the Llibeth Forrest—look for the largest tree—I will be there.”

“Be safe Fletcher.”

“And you.”

Zion lifted me onto the horse. A moment later, I left Zion with the boy. Wasgo and I set off at a fast clip, eager to reach the Aligeri Mountains and Plata’s Peak. I didn’t look back. I knew I wouldn’t be able to leave Zion if I did. I hoped he would find, and rescue, Alisa.

PLATA'S PEAK

For several hours, I rode the horse at a trot along the road heading northwest. I wasn't concerned about riding in the dark. I finally found my courage, dug my heels in, and pushed the mare to a gallop.

After a few hours of riding, Wasgo and I stopped where the road forked at a mill. I slid off the horse and tied it to a tree. Pulling out Marcus's map, I tried to figure out which direction to go.

"The road forks here," I said to Wasgo, pointing out the location on the map. "The road to the right takes up right past a Fetcher's camp but it ends right near Plata's Peak. The other circles round the back side, but it's the long way." I looked at Wasgo. "Which way should we go?"

Wasgo looked up at me. "We go right and hope we don't get caught."

I nodded. We turned right, traveled over the bridge, and continued down the cart path towards the camp. We quietly circled round the camp avoiding any guards and continued down the cart path. After several more behind-numbing hours of riding, the trees thinned out and narrowed into a footpath.

By now, the faint sunlight filtered over the mountaintops as the morning waned. The path turned west, and we followed it through some narrows between two mountains. Claustrophobia set in. I was beginning to wonder if we would ever come out when we finally exited out the other side. The pathway ended with a grand valley opened before us.

"I guess this is where the path ends." Wasgo said, stating the obvious.

"Yeah, and that must be Plata's Peak." I said, pointing to the tallest peak between two mountains in front of us.

"We have to climb that and find the artifact?" I questioned aloud.

"Not we . . . you."

I looked down at Wasgo.

"Paws, my friend," he said. "Not meant for climbing."

"You could morph," I said.

"Oh no, this one is all yours—I don't do heights."

"Great, you're no help."

"I'll go with you as far as I can."

"Thanks."

I pointed the horse straight at Plata's Peak and dug my heels in its side.

ROCK CLIMBING

It was amazing! The horse sprinted full speed across the valley. At first, it was all I could do to hold onto the reins without falling off. Then, as we crossed the plain, I settled into the saddle and found my rhythm with its strides. I felt its power underneath my seat as we rushed across the wild grass.

We came to a halt on the far side of the valley, and the peak looming over us.

"How am I going to climb that thing?" I asked Wasgo.

"How do you eat an antelope?" he asked.

"I don't know?"

"One bite at a time," he said, and howled.

"Very funny."

"I thought so too."

"Let's get going."

I hopped off the horse and let it wander off in the valley. I didn't want to tie it down in case I didn't make it back; I couldn't stomach the thought that it would be stuck to the rock and die of starvation.

Wasgo and I started our climb. It was easy going at first. For several hours, we picked our way around boulders, always moving up the side of the mountain. The temperature dropped the higher we climbed. I was glad it was midsummer and there was not as much snow on the mountain, but it was still icy in places.

"Let's go around to the south side of the mountain," I said.

Wasgo nodded.

The south side was less steep than the north, and I saw a crack that I could wedge myself between to climb up to a platform a quarter of the way up the face of the top of Plata's Peak. We rounded the side of the mountain to get to it. Wasgo slipped on some loose rocks and rolled twenty feet down the side amid an avalanche of small debris. He landed with a yelp against a boulder. It was a good thing, too, or he would have kept rolling several hundred feet more. I descended in a cautious slide down to where he lay.

"Are you all right?"

"Yes," he said, and licked the red fur on his front leg near his paw.

"I think this is where I leave you," I said. "Head back down and keep an eye on my horse. I don't know if I'll be coming back down this way."

"Really?"

"Let's just say that it's a suspicion I have, based on something my friend Marcus Dunn said to me."

"Oh. . . okay, then," Wasgo said, standing up. "Be safe, my friend."

I watched Wasggo limp back down the mountain. When he disappeared, I turned, and continued along the base of the tall granite face to the crevice I had seen. I heard something crunch under my foot, and I looked down. I was standing on the arm of a skeleton. I saw that the bone on the one side of the skull was crushed flat. I looked around me and saw another body twenty feet away. This one was more recent. It lay in an awkward position, but I was able to make out a Fetcher's shirt.

A huge knot of fear grew in my gut. It felt as if one of these boulders was materializing in the pit of my stomach. It didn't go away after swallowing hard. I stared up at the impossibly steep crags facing me; I didn't want to end up like one of these guys.

Needing some reassurance before my climb, I took the tablet out and read the words again. "BELIEF." "STRENGTH." "COURAGE." Then, I read the final inscription, "RESOLVE".

> *Fortitude is not enough when you act.*
> *Intent. Direction. Firmness of purpose.*
> *Your mind must make one way or the other.*
> *What is hard if your intention is soft?*
> *Decide on it and make it become real.*
> *Take action and go forward with RESOLVE.*

I realized why this one was last. You needed belief, strength, and courage to have resolve in the face of tough challenges. Right now, I am faced with two decisions. I could walk away and head back down the mountain with Wasgo, or I could continue to climb this mountain, even though I might fall to my death in the attempt—either way, my decision to give up, or not give up, needed to be resolute.

I put the tablet back in my satchel, twisted it more securely around my back, and began the climb until I came to a rock wall with a crack in the middle. With a hand and a foot on each side of the crack, I inched my way up like a monkey, climbing with ease. At about thirty feet high, I looked down. Big mistake.

Unease set in as I realized that I was already high enough to break my neck if I fell. I pressed on, finally gaining the relative safety of my new perch. I pulled myself up over the edge and slid on my rear until my back was against the rock wall. The view was amazing. I could see over the hills, across the forest, all the way to the sea. Mount Norchet stood on my right, the mines on my left, and San Fargo straight ahead, off in the distance. A treetop poked above the others in the middle of the forest.

"That must be the World Tree," I whispered in the breeze.

Finding a new energy from within, I stood up, and turned to face my newest challenge. I looked up the cliff face, searching for a way to climb it. I noticed a small ledge that started waist-high, angled up in a slight incline, and disappeared around the corner.

It was slow going. I had to find nearly non-existent grips within an arm's reach, in order to be able to slide my feet forward without falling backwards. After inching along the ledge for some time, I realized that I was directly above the spot where I found the two bodies. They must have made it this far as well, only to have fallen to their deaths.

Panic raced through my body. I froze. Helpless, I started to focus on my physical discomfort; my fingers burned; my toes ached in my boots from balancing on the ledge; I felt the weight of the tablet in my satchel become heavier as the invisible force of gravity pulled it towards the rocks below, inviting me to go with it.

Was this what Marcus was hinting at? Was I going to fall?

Then the words on the tablet slammed into my fears.

Go forward with BELIEF.

I needed to have the belief that I would succeed.

Go forward with STRENGTH.

I needed strength to hang on.

Go forward with COURAGE.

I needed courage to continue along this lip.

Go forward with RESOLVE.

I needed to be determined that I was not going to fall. I needed to be determined that I would make it to the top.

Marcus's words ran through my head. *Don't be afraid to fall.*

"Yeah right!" I said to the air. "What does he know?"

I was, understandably, completely scared of falling. How could you not be afraid of falling when there are boulders waiting to greet you a thousand feet below?

Fighting off the fatigue in my left arm, I pulled myself onto a sloped ledge. I stood there, shaking with fright. This was not going well. I had to find a way up, or I would have to climb back down. I didn't know if I had enough oomph left in me to make it back the way I came—let alone make it to the top even if there was a way up.

After my heart stopped pounding in my ears, I gathered my wits and looked at the granite wall before me. I scanned the entire rock face for hand and foot holds, or any way at all to make it to the top.

"Nothing?"

There was not a single crack or ledge to use to traverse the remaining distance.

"Great!"

I lowered my head and thought about what I could do. There was no choice but to go back.

I don't think I can do it.

My hands started trembling.

It took most of my energy to get to this point.

My knees started shaking.

I can't stay here on the shelf.

I had to go back.

I wonder if this is why the others fell. Did they slip off the ledge where I almost did? Did they climb back down and not make it?

I don't know if I can do this.

My teeth started chattering from the cold.

What did the tablet say about resolve?

You must make up your mind one way or another.

If I go back, I might fall. If I stay here, I will surely fall. Either way I have to come to grips with falling. However, with the latter I will have a chance of making it down alive.

After a half hour of slowly making my way down, my hands and toes were giving out, and what little strength I still possessed was leaving me. I couldn't go any further.

Don't be afraid to fall.

Marcus's words bounced in my head again. For some reason, that didn't sound too bad. My hands and forearms burned, and my toes felt like they were going to break off.

Don't be afraid to fall.

Tired, cold, windblown, and out of strength I froze on the granite wall. Paralyzed, and unable to move any further, I succumbed to Marcus's words, let go, and fell backwards.

Falling.

Falling.

BLUE SKY

This is it! I thought. I am done for!

Even though my arms flailed in the air, my feet kicked violently as I fell, and a scream blasted out of my mouth, my mind was strangely clear. I noticed the oddest things: the dazzling blue sky; the tendril whips of clouds that streaked across the sky, flowing with purpose in a symbiotic dance with the periwinkle above, and I thought about my life.

It is crazy how your whole life flashes before you when you know you are going to die. I reminisced about the past few days; Zion, Alisa, Wasgo, Marcus. I hoped they would be all right. I thought about my parents. *Where are they? What are they doing?* Then the Prime Ministerial and the Oraculum flashed in my mind with their sinister grins mocking me. I heard their laughter in the wind.

I felt something hit my body like a ton of bricks. Whatever it was, it squeezed around my chest, it knocked the air completely out of me, and I passed out.

THE EAGLE'S NEST

I came to with a rush of air in my lungs while staring at the claws of a giant bird. They were wrapped around my body so firmly I couldn't move an inch. I could barely breathe.

Gently, I turned my head and saw the cliffs of Plata's Peak below me. I saw Wasgo and the horse. They were two specks in the valley below. I was soaring through the sky.

The feeling of flying was indescribable; having never done it before, I had no words for it, and it was so very different from falling. I felt safe for the moment, but I knew I would be in for big problems once we landed somewhere.

I knew the satchel was still on my back because it was cutting into my neck as it dangled and swung about freely. I just hoped that all the artifacts remained in their pockets.

The giant bird circled on the thermals, then nosedived towards Plata's Peak heading down towards a giant nest built the crook of a rock on the tip of the peak. As we swooped in, its giant wings extended and beat downward, bringing us to a halt a few inches above the nest.

The bird released its grip on me. I tumbled out onto

the mass of woven branches, twigs, and feathers, and came to a halt, face to face with a sun-bleached human skull. I knew I had to act quickly, or my fate would be the same.

Pulling out the tablet, I spun around to face the bird, backed against the far lip of the nest and used it as a shield.

I stared down a giant Golden Eagle who was eyeing me as dinner. I didn't know what was worse, falling to your death or being ripped to bits by an Eagle. Neither of them I wanted to experience, so I yelled at Eagle, hoping it would fly off and I could figure out a way safely off this peak.

Eagle didn't move. I slowly reached a hand into one of the many pockets of the satchel and grabbed the corkscrew. I positioned the handle in my palm, with the metal tip protruding through my fingers. I would use it as a weapon if I could.

Eagle attacked. It flew into the air and swiped at me with its claws. Although the stone tablet did a good job blocking the raptor's swipes, one of its blows managed to hit me in the shoulder, and I flew across the nest.

Eagle hopped over to where I lay. Rolling onto my back, I held the tablet in front of my chest as it poked at me with its beak. Feinting to the side, I jabbed the tip of the corkscrew into its leg.

Eagle shrieked and flew back a few feet. It shrieked a second time, and attacked me again, with full vengeance. Its beak hit the tablet repeatedly. I was afraid the tablet was going to break at any moment, and I would be done for. With a lucky stride, the beak poked into the center hole of the tablet and came millimeters from my chest. I held on as hard as I could as it tried to free itself.

The sun glinted off the metal of the corkscrew and

the reflection flashed in both our eyes. The binding light stopped Eagle's attack for a moment.

I slid the tablet off the curve of its beak and scooted back against the edge of the nest.

Eagle stared at me and blinked.

It looked at me then at my hand.

"Oh, you saw this?" I said, standing.

I held the corkscrew up, so it flashed in the sunlight again.

Eagle screeched and flapped its wings.

I flinched backwards.

Eagle hopped over to the side of the nest, scraped at the side with its claw and then dug its beak in amongst the twigs as it was searching for something. A moment later, it pulled out a gold feather.

I stood there in disbelief.

Eagle hopped over to me, dropped the feather at my feet. It bowed its head to me.

"The artifact," I said. "You are the protector of the artifact."

It blinked its affirmation.

The intelligence in its eyes told me it wouldn't attack again so I reached out and stroked its beak.

"Thank you."

I put the tablet and the corkscrew away before picking up the gold feather. Looking it over, I realized that it was made of pure gold. When I ran it through my fingers, the vane of it revealed the pattern of the world tree. I knew I had found the final artifact.

I placed it into my bag with everything else. As adrenaline ceased to flow through my body, my teeth began to chatter, and I shuddered from the cold as it seeped into me through my shirt. I couldn't stay up here much longer without freezing to death.

"How do I get off this mountain?" I asked Eagle.

It raised its wings.

"Right, of course," I said, "Fly."

It hopped up next to me.

"You'd let me ride you?"

It blinked.

I secured my satchel, hopped onto its back, and held on for dear life as Eagle lifted off and flew me into the air.

For the second time that day I flew.

FLYING

I had thought sitting a horse at full speed was exhilarating but flying on the back of a giant eagle was ten times more exciting. I felt Eagle's power beneath my legs as it flapped its wings, and we caught a thermal to ride. Spreading its wings, we floated weightless as a leaf on the current of wind. I thought I would feel scared looking down at the mountains and valley below from this height, but I found that I felt confident and alive, soaring across the sky.

We circled Plata's Peak at about seven thousand feet. From this viewpoint, I understood why they called it Plata's Peak. Plata is an old word for plate. Each side of the peak had flat granite walls, but that is not why it was called Plata. Rather, the name came from the top, which was shaped like a square plate that curved up at the edges. It was the perfect place for a giant eagle to make its nest.

As we circled down, I saw the ledge where I had slipped and almost met my doom. I looked past the ledge to the surface beyond, and realized it was a completely flat rock with no lip to stand on or cracks to wedge between. There wouldn't have been anywhere for me to go even if I had tried.

We turned away from the mountain and headed to

the north tip of the valley. The next moment we were diving. I hunched into Eagle's body as cold air rushed past my body. I could hear nothing but the whistling of wind as my stomach rode up into my throat. Eagle leveled off when we were about twenty feet over the wild grass floor of the valley. We must have been traveling at least ten times faster than the horse. It was thrilling to see the ground blur behind us and the mountainous landscape on either side rushing past as Eagle flapped its wings, keeping our momentum.

As we passed the Fetcher camp, I waved the golden feather I had retrieved from my satchel, and shouted, "I found the last artifact!"

I wanted them to know that they were free from their life's duty. I secured the feather in its place inside my satchel. When we reached the southern end of the valley, Eagle changed direction yet again, and headed straight up into the air, gaining several thousand feet in altitude before banking again. That moment in which it turned held a feeling of weightlessness that I had never experienced before—I almost lost my grip on its neck feathers.

Eagle pulled its wings in and went into freefall. Dropping like a bullet out of the sky, my stomach lurched into my throat. I felt like I was falling off the ledge again. At the last second, Eagle extended its wings, caught the air and we rushed over the plain again.

We passed the camp again. Every Fetcher was out in the valley when we passed the second time. They cheered. Halfway along the valley Eagle opened its wings wide, flapped a few times as if back-pedaling, hovered in midair, then landed on its feet in the grass. It seemed so effortless.

"That was awesome!" I yelled exuberantly and

hopped off its back. "I would love to do that again."

"Maybe sometime," it said, in its screechy voice.

I was not shocked that it could talk. In the past few days, I had talked to several animals—of course, that could have been my imagination run amok, but I didn't think that was the case.

When I looked away from Eagle, I saw my friends approaching.

"You made it back alive," Wasgo said.

"Barely," I replied. "I fell off the cliff. If it wasn't for eagle catching me, I wouldn't be standing here."

"Well, here you are," Eagle interjected.

"Yes, but not until after you tried to impale me with your beak," I said,

Eagle and I chuckled—if you call an Eagle screech a chuckle.

"You did it," Panther said.

"You found all of the artifacts," Moose added.

"Now you must go to the World Tree," Bear finished.

"What happens at the World Tree?"

"You will figure it out," said Bear.

"I am sure I will."

I whistled and the horse came galloping up a moment later. I mounted the horse with ease and headed out of the valley the way we had come. This time I had five companions with me.

A STANDOFF

We traveled through the narrows to the ravine, and down the path to the mill. Several hundred Fetchers and a half dozen Ministerial Guards met us on the bridge.

"We will take the artifacts." One of the guards informed me.

"You can try," I said confidently, as my friends stood next to me.

Bear stood upright on his haunches, Panther growled and crouched into attack position, Moose lowered his antlers ready to charge, Wasgo snarled and arched his back, and Eagle landed on the roof of the mill scratching his talons on the slate roof.

"Fellow Fetchers," I said, addressing the crowd, "you are all free to go now."

They stood on the bridge, confused, looking at one another, not knowing what to do. I understood what they were thinking and feeling. Their entire lives, like me, they had lived as Fetchers, and they knew nothing else—it was their life job—their life's purpose.

"We have nowhere to go," one man said.

A little girl stepped from the crowd and walked up to me. She wore an oversized Fetcher's shirt with a belt wrapped around her waist, making it into a dress.

"This is for you," she said, handing me a bracelet,

"for finding the artifacts.'

"Thank you," I replied.

She tied the bracelet around my wrist.

"What is it made out of?" I asked her.

"I made it with scraps of shirts from the Fetchers at the mountain."

I pondered what she had said, and my eyes began to tear. Many Fetchers had lost their lives looking for the artifacts now cradled in my satchel. Looking at her, and the others, I was humbled, and fiercely proud of the people I was once part of. My heart was glad that I had found this group before they had been harmed. No more Fetchers would sacrifice their lives in search of artifacts.

"We are heading to the World Tree." I addressed the Fetchers.

"We will follow you," she said.

"I'll lead the way," Bear whispered, lowering himself back down on all fours.

He stepped off the path and rambled through the underbrush. Moose and the other animals followed Bear trampling down the bushes, making a trail for us to follow.

I, along with two hundred or so of my brethren traipsed through the forest to find the World Tree.

Later, I glanced back and saw the Ministerial Guards following at the rear. They must have come to the same conclusion that the Fetchers had; now that the artifacts had been found, their purpose had ended. So, they too followed.

THE WORLD TREE

Yggdrasil. Tree of Life. Goah's tree. World Tree. Whatever you call it, it is the largest tree in the forest. Supposedly, it has healing properties, gives everlasting life, or grants ultimate power. Many had sought it, but none had ever found it. People would travel the forest for days, unknowingly coming close, but the magic and mysticism of the tree was such that it would keep them from finding it.

I knew, on this day, we would find it. What I didn't know was what would happen when we did.

After traveling several hours, we stepped out of the dense trees into a large clearing. A single, massive tree grew in the center. The trunk, which had a golden sheen to its grainy surface, was so large that I figured it would take a hundred or more people holding hands to encircle its base. The branches of the great tree stretched overhead, forming a roof as they touched and entwined with the trees of the surrounding forest. Even though we were in a clearing, we were sheltered completely by the canopy of leaves.

"This is so amazing," the tiny voice next to me said.

The girl was right. It was something out of a dream. I looked up at the silver leaves, and a silent breeze moved them slightly, causing them to shimmer in the afternoon sun. Thin rays from the sun reflected and filtered through the top of the tree and trickled down in a soft iridescent glow.

I felt something inside of me come alive. It was a feeling I couldn't explain but it was a silent connection as I felt the presence of some magical force or presence coming from the tree. Then, I remembered—Goah.

He was here—in this tree. I felt it.

"Well done, Fletcher!" a familiar voice said behind me. "You made all this possible."

Breaking the perfection of the moment, I turned to face the voice.

"Prime Ministerial," I said, not surprised he was here.

He stood near the edge of the forest, holding on to Alisa's shoulders, her arms bound behind her. The Oraculum stood next to him.

"You have something I want."

"What is it you want?" I asked, knowing full well what it was.

"I want to make a trade," he replied.

A moment later, Zion stepped from the forest, came over, and stood next to me.

"Sorry, they grabbed her away from me," Zion said.

"That's okay, we'll get her back," I whispered, then turned my attention back to the Prime Ministerial. "What do you want to trade for?"

"The girl . . . for the artifacts."

I looked at Zion. He shook his head with disbelief that this was happening to him and his daughter. I could tell he was torn between his daughter's life and the artifacts affecting the fate of the world.

Zion sighed and whispered, "Don't give up the artifacts."

I nodded. "No. I will not give them to you," I stated, calling the Prime Ministrial's bluff.

"You will. The Oraculum has seen it. In fact, you will hand over a certain bottle . . . One with the world tree on it."

"Don't do it Fletcher," Zion said.

"But Alisa?"

"I will get her out of this—somehow," Zion said, cracking his knuckles, ready to bull rush the Prime Ministerial.

"Don't Zion." I said, "They will strike you down before you get halfway to her."

I quickly ran through the other possibilities: Zion could rush forward to save his daughter, but the Ministerial Guard would strike him down to protect the Prime Ministerial; Wasgo, Moose, Bear, Panther, or Eagle could attack the Prime Ministerial, but that too was risky—Alisa may get hurt in the process; I could run, but with the Ministerial Guard everywhere, they would eventually find me and get the artifacts anyway.

Come on Goah do something! I thought.

Moments ticked by and nothing happened. Not a sign, not a peep came from Goah. I would have to give the bottle up. Then I remembered what Wasgo had said to me at the beginning of this adventure. What if this was what I was supposed to do? Maybe the Oracullum saw something that they hadn't told the Prime Ministerial. Maybe I had to have the belief to hand it over. Besides, I still had the other artifacts. I could still run.

"Hurry up boy!" said the Prime Ministerial, squeezing Alisa's shoulders. He was getting impatient. "I don't have all day to stand here."

"Ouch," said Alisa looking at him crossly.

"If you don't give me the bottle *now*, I will take it by

force!"

"Okay, you can have it."

"Fletcher, you can't give him the artifacts," said Zion.

"It's all right Zion," I said. "I have to get your daughter back."

"I know, but the artifacts—"

"Besides, he only asked for the bottle—not *all* the artifacts. You will have to have belief that this will work out."

I took the cobalt bottle out of its pocket and handed it to the little girl. "Give this to the Prime Ministerial," I said.

She took the bottle, walked over to the Prime Ministerial, and gingerly handed it to him. The Prime Ministerial grabbed the bottle from her, smiled triumphantly at me, and pushed Alisa away from him.

Zion rushed forward to grab her, but one of the Oraculum got to her first.

"It is mine now!" the Prime Ministerial cried.

Holding the bottle in both hands, he broke the seal with his teeth, spit out the waxy substance, and lifted it to his lips. He took a sip and swallowed. Seconds later, his face, neck and face turned gray. He dropped the bottle, clutched his throat, A dark smoke exited his mouth and flew into the air towards the Oraculum.

The Prime Ministerial looked confused. He peered around at all the Fetchers before him. "What happened? Where am I? What's going on?" The Prime Ministerial dropped the bottle and he fell limp to the ground, unconscious.

The smoke split then absorbed into the Oraculums bodies.

THE KEY TO THE TREE

The Fetcher girl was quick. She grabbed the falling bottle out of the air, rushed it over, and gently handed it to me, careful not to get any liquid on herself.

The other Oraculum stepped over the body of the Prime Ministerial.

"The fool," The one holding onto Alisa said.

"I saw that coming," the other said.

"He's out of our way now," the first Oraculum replied.

"Now, you will do as we say," both Oraculum said in unison.

"Okay," I replied. "Don't hurt her."

"Take the tablet out. Lay it on the ground. Dip the feather into the liquid in the bottle and drip the liquid into the channel etched in the center of the tablet. Then, dump the rest of the liquid into the outer channel."

Holding the bottle upright, so I wouldn't spill any, I took the tablet out of my satchel with my free hand and laid it on the ground. I took out the gold feather, dipped it in the remaining liquid in the bottle, and held it over the channel around the center of the tablet. As the droplets hit the granite, I felt a surge of power from the tree. The droplets shimmered and revealed hidden letters in the channel. I dumped the remaining liquid in the bottle into the groove etched around the edge of the tablet.

After a moment, words appeared within that channel of the tablet as well.

"What does it say?" they said, unblinking.

I was not surprised they knew what to do with the liquid. The one Oraculum was a seer, like Marcus, and had most likely seen all of this in a vision.

"It reads; 'With BELIEF, place the tablet in the knots of the tree. Take the corkscrew and, in the center hole of the tablet, screw it into the tree. Pull with all your STRENGTH. As the spirit water flows from the tree, fill the bottle. Speak your desire, and with COURAGE, take a drink. If you have the RESOLVE to do so, your intentions will be fulfilled.'"

"Let's get on with it," said the Oraculum.

I looked at Alisa in their grasp and knew I had to do it, or they would hurt her. I dumped the liquid off the tablet and stepped up to the tree trunk. Walking around the enormous expanse, I inspected its rough surface for the knots the tablet referenced.

When I had circled it completely, the knots appeared where I had started.

Those weren't there before.

I fit the tablet in the ridges of the knots; they held the tablet by the corners, perfectly. I took the corkscrew and twisted it into the tree. With both hands, I yanked.

Nothing happened.

I put one foot on the tree and pulled it again.

Nothing.

I pulled on the corkscrew and placed both feet on the tree trunk and pulled with all my might.

The bark gave way, and I went flying backwards.

I knew landing on my back was going to hurt so I

closed my eyes, prepared for the impact. A half second later my back hit, but it wasn't the hard ground I expected.

"Hello, Fletcher," a familiar voice said.

I opened my eyes and looked into Pale blue eyes. I had known these eyes for years.

"Marcus?"

Marcus, who had caught me midair, set me on my feet. I spun around to face him, but it wasn't him. I mean, it wasn't the Marcus I knew.

This Marcus was cleanly shaven and had his normally unkempt hair parted nicely and combed back. He wore a white collared shirt under a crimson red smoking jacket that hung down over tan slacks. This wasn't the Marcus I knew. This was most unusual.

"Wait a minute," I said. "You look familiar. You're . . ."

"Lorucias Guifachs."

Everyone stood rooted in place, staring in awe. That is, everyone except the Oraculum.

"How is that possible?" I asked. "You should be over one hundred by now."

"One hundred and ten…" he said. "The spider bite altered me, and I don't age the same as you.".

"Fletcher," the Oraculum interrupted. "Bring us a bottle of the spirit water.'

I looked at Marcus . . . Lorucias.

He nodded. "It's all right Fletcher. Have belief my friend."

I took the bottle to the tree that now had a small fountain of water flowing from it, filled it to the top with spirit water, and walked it over to the Oraculum.

The seer grabbed the bottle, and the doer pushed Alisa to the side.

"This is it," they said in unison. "This is what we have been waiting for all these years."

The Oraculum faced each other, and both held on to the bottle. "We wish for eternal youth." First one took a drink then the other.

After a few seconds passed by, they held out their hands.

"We are starting to feel younger."

"Brother, your face looks younger."

"Wait a minute!" the seer shouted. "Brother, you are getting shorter."

"So are you!"

"I think we are getting much younger."

In a matter of seconds, the Oraculum went from being full-grown men, to youthful teenagers, children, then finally, crying infants.

"I saw this moment, but I didn't really expect it to end like that for them—I guess they got what they asked for."

"Yeah, eternal youth!" I replied.

Alisa and Zion stepped up next to us.

"Fletcher what happened?" she asked.

"Well, let's say I took a gamble, and it paid off."

"They certainly didn't see that coming," Zion interjected.

Alisa looked at me out of the corner of her eye and I knew she wanted more of an explanation than that.

"I remembered Marcus telling me that when he had dreams or visions of what was to happen, they were sometimes unclear. I hoped that the Oracullum hadn't seen exactly what was etched in the tablet under the liquid, and I changed a part of it on the fly. The tablet said to fill your hands with liquid and drink, not drink from the bottle."

"Nice one Fletcher," Alisa said, and gave me a high five.

"That was a big risk," Zion said.

"I knew I had them when they ignored what had just happened to the Prime Ministerial. The remnants of the liquid in the bottle corrupted the spirit water just enough to change them into that."

We looked over to the drooling babies that were now crawling naked on the pile of Oracullum clothes.

"Hello, my old friend," Lorucias said, as Wasgo approached, with the other animals.

Wasgo rubbed his side against Lorucias's leg.

Lorucias scratched Wasgo's head, between his ears.

"Wait a minute," I said. "You both were in on this.'

"Woof."

"Yep," an unrepentant Lorucias said. "Now, you have something to finish." He pointed to the World Tree.

I stepped up to the small fountain flowing from the tree through the center of the tablet. Wasgo, Lorucias, Zion, Alisa, the guardian animals, and all the Fetchers crowded around with great interest.

I thought about the best gift I could wish for, that would help everyone, not just me.

I formed a bowl with my hands and filled it with spirit water.

"I wish for . . . *freedom*. Freedom for my fellow Fetchers and all the people of Danforth." I said and took a drink.

The sliver tree shimmered and engulfed everyone in a dazzling flash of light.

FREEDOM

As the light from the tree faded, I stepped to the trunk and pushed the diamond into the hole. The spirit water stopped flowing and the tree started to shake violently.

We all backed away to the safety of the trees surrounding the clearing. Rays of light shot out from the diamond in all directions. We covered our eyes. When the rays subsided, we looked to where the World Tree had stood. In its place sat a small white dove.

The dove winked and flew straight up into the sky disappearing in the sunlight.

As it flew into the sky, I was filled with the knowledge that my people were free. I knew that we were able to choose our own path and not have to live a destiny that was chosen for us by some Oracullum. We could go where we want. Learn new things. And be who we want to be."

"What is it, Fletcher?" Lorucias asked. "You look overwhelmed."

"Yeah, I kind of am," I replied. "For the first time in my life, I don't know what I am supposed to do."

"I know I want to explore," said Lorucias. "I heard the world is round, not flat, and possibly has many other continents on it to explore."

"That all sounds interesting," I said. "Why don't

you?"

"Maybe I will."

Wasgo padded over to me and morphed into his spirit guide form one last time. The Fetchers standing near jumped with shock to see him change form.

"Fletcher, your journey is complete," he said. "You can change the world now and make it better."

"But I don't know what to do first," I said, unsure of my purpose.

"With your newfound freedom, I am sure you will figure it out," Wasgo said. "Now, go lead your people out of here."

"But the ministerial?"

"They won't be an issue anymore."

"What?"

"They will have a new purpose," said Wasgo.

He turned and stepped up next to Zion Johnson then addressed the crowd of Fetchers and Ministerial Guards.

"This man has shown great courage and strength throughout this journey. He demonstrated his willingness to put others before himself and protect those he knew little about. Those are qualities of a great leader." Wasgo paused a moment to let that sink in. "Does anyone here oppose the election of Zion Johnson as your new Prime Ministerial?"

"I don't," said Lorucias.

"No," shouted a Fetcher from the back.

No," said a Ministerial Guard next to me.

"If none are opposed, Zion Johnson is your new Prime Ministerial!"

The crowd erupted with cheers and great elation.

Zion looked at Wasgo as if he didn't believe what was happening. Alisa grabbed his hand and squeezed it.

"Ministerial Guards come forth," Wasgo commanded as the cheering subsided.

All guards stepped forward in a semicircle before Wasgo. "From this day forward, this man is your leader. Do you swear to protect him from harm and uphold the laws of Danforth and to serve and protect the true and just people of this world?"

"We do!" they all replied.

Wasgo stared at them sternly as he examined their intention individually.

"Good. I believe you will. Now, it is your duty to tell all other Ministerial Guards of this new-world order and that it is their duty to serve and protect the free people of Danforth as decreed on this fine day."

Wasgo turned to Lorucias, "My job is done, I must go home now."

"Will we see you again?" I asked.

"I will always be with you in your heart," he said, pointing at his chest.

"I figured he would say something like that," Lorucias said.

We all chuckled.

"Go forward and learn, Fletcher" he said, and changed into wolf form.

Wasgo turned and walked away. Eagle flew off, and Moose, Panther, and Bear crossed the clearing with him. Before they came to the edge of the clearing, they looked back, winked then disappeared into the trees.

Tears flowed down my cheeks. I had a feeling that I would never see them again. I turned to my friends, the Fetchers, and the Ministerial Guard who were all staring at me. I picked up the four artifacts, along with the tablet, and placed them safely in my satchel.

"Let's go home!" I said.

EPILOGUE

Today is the tenth anniversary of *World Tree Day*—the celebration of the day that changed everything in the world. The celebration is much different from Guifachs Night. During the day, we share books and stories, and I give a speech in the town hall. At night, the city streets come alive as lanterns light up the wall. People from all over Danforth take to the streets with music and food. The Festival of Freedom culminates with a final fireworks display and the releasing of a dove.

I hoped to see Lorucias tonight and thank him for giving me the idea, on our walk back from the World Tree ten years ago, of what to do with San Fargo. I haven't seen him in those ten years. He bought a frigate and has sailed the seas in search of new lands.

"What are you going to do with your freedom?" he had asked.

"I don't know," I replied. "I have been a Fetcher all my life."

"What are all the Fetchers going to do now?"

"I'm not sure."

"Why don't you create an institute of higher learning and tradesmanship?"

It was a brilliant idea. I wasn't sure why I hadn't thought of it myself. People can learn what they want and build their own future.

The day of our return, I set up the top room of the bell tower as my office, and opened several classrooms around the city, which have since expanded to several hundred classrooms. Alisa and I have grown close over the years. We each have a room in the bell tower and spend much time together, planning and creating. When I am not teaching and training, we walk the walls or sit by the river talking and just hanging out together.

A week ago, Zion Johnson informed me of a special ceremony to take place on the Tenth Anniversary Celebration and asked me to share my story there. With that as motivation, I sit now, to write everything exactly how it happened, down to the last detail. I remember my adventure as if it was only yesterday, and I want to write while the memories are fresh. In this way, we will keep the story alive. For generations to come, it will be read during the day of the celebration. I am so excited to give it to the university tonight—it is going to be a special day in more ways than one.

I dip the tip of the golden feather into the ink that now resides in the blue bottle, scribble the last words in this book to complete my story, and head down for the final feast before the fireworks.

I climb the ladder to the bell and give it a healthy tug, signaling the start of our meal. With the echo of the bell still ringing in the streets, I make my way to the great hall, with the bound parchment papers that hold my story clasped snugly against my side.

Several hundred pairs of eyes shift attention to me as I walk past their tables to the front where I stand at the podium that now holds the crest of San Fargo proudly carved into its surface. The Fetcher's creed is still in its place of honor on the wall.

I see Zion and Alisa in the front row. Shortly after, Lorucias and a wolf come through the door to the hall and sit down in the back. I am excited to see them both.

A warmth spreads over me as I place the parchment on the podium. I feel Goah with me. I choke back the emotions that threaten to surface and begin reading.

All are silent and still.

"It was once said you could be anything you want to be in life. You could be a butcher, a baker, or a candlestick maker. You could make your own destiny. However, in our world, in this age, your destiny is chosen for you."

I took a sip of water and continued. "But all that changed ten years ago. This is the story of how things came to be."

The crowd on the streets had heard what was happening and they filed into the hall, standing in the aisles, and poking their heads through the windows to hear me read the pages of my journey. In certain parts, I turn and read the inscriptions on the tablet that I had mounted on the wall behind me.

When finished reading, I stopped and cleared my throat to address the group.

"That week taught me a lot of things—especially there at the end."

They all laugh.

"Mostly I learned about the human spirit, and how oppression, seclusion, and tyranny cannot keep free will down. Eventually, the people will rise and prevail against tyranny. You see, it is having belief, strength, courage, and resolve that make it happen. As you can see from my story, and as you sit here today, you are all exercising your free will as you see fit. Fetchers as well as people all over the world come here to seek knowledge, higher learning, and practice trades of their own choosing—no longer are they told what they will be in life. With that, my fellow Fetchers, and good people of San Fargo, go forward with FREEDOM.

There are claps and cheers throughout the streets of San Fargo.

"Thank you," I say, raising my hands to hush the crowd. "I have one more thing—Alisa, would you join me up here?"

Alisa looks at her father, then at me, obviously wondering what is going on. Finally, she walks up to the front of the room.

"Alisa," I say, taking hold of her hands. "From the day we first met in the tent, through the days that followed, and throughout the last ten years, you have been by my side." I drop to one knee and take a ring out of my pocket. "Will you be by my side forever?"

I held the ring out to her.

"Will you marry me?"

She looks at me, then her dad, then back to me again in disbelief.

"Yes." she says, taking the ring. "Yes, I will!"

I stood up and we hugged as the room erupted in cheers again.

"I am sorry it's not as big as the diamond we found in the mine."

She laughs.

"It did come from the same chamber though."

"It's beautiful."

Prime Ministerial Zion Johnson stands, steps forward, and places a hand on my shoulder.

"Thank you, Fletcher Barnes, for your words of inspiration to all generations to come—and congratulations to the two of you!"

He squeezes my shoulder and I give him a nod.

"Now, I have an important announcement," he says hushing everyone. "Well, two actually—I want to announce that from this day forward, San Fargo will be officially known as San Fargo University, which I am pleased to say is the first of its kind in this world!"

Everyone claps and cheers again.

"Hold on," he says, holding up his hand. "That's not all. I personally name Fletcher Barnes as Headmaster of San Fargo University, to hire and train professors of learning and skill, from all walks of life, to help him pass on his teachings."

Lorucias stands, "Here's to Fletcher, the true Headmaster of San Fargo!"

I receive a standing ovation as the hall overflows with sounds of jubilation. I had never felt happier in my life, and I know that this is what I am supposed to be doing—helping other people.

As the excitement subsides, Zion speaks again, "Fetcher, what do you say—do you accept?"

"I am honored to be your Headmaster. But I want everyone to remember . . ." I paused and looked out on my fellow Fetchers. "I am, and always will be a Fetcher."

"Now you are the Headmaster... a Fetcher of knowledge!" Alisa interjects.

"Yes . . . a Fetcher of knowledge." I repeated.

Then it hit me. I am a Fetcher and will always be a Fetcher.

SAN FARGO
UNIVERSITY

ACKNOWLEDGMENTS

I want to thank Cael Johnson for bringing these chapters to life with his wonderful illustrations. Your work is amazing. I appreciate you helping me make the words and images in my head come to life with your creative illustrations throughout this book. You are an amazing artist and I hope you soar to great heights. Thanks for working on this project.

ABOUT THE AUTHOR

As a child, Tim Northburg loved to act out adventures with his friends. In the park, he played the roles of a British spy, a hero in a galaxy far away, or a brave Knight of the round table. Many years later when reading his children, the bedtime stories he loved as a kid, it sparked his wondrous imagination from his childhood. He started writing down those ideas and they turned into several books and screenplays in various genres. Tim loves to write from the imagination he had as a child and enjoys the opportunity to share it with others. It is his goal to inspire people of all ages to use their imagination to reach their dreams.

www.TimNorthburg.com

ABOUT THE ARTIST

Cael Johnson is a freelance digital artist from Durban, South Africa who mostly draws fantasy characters with a strong African influence in a quirky, cartoon style. He specializes in concept art, character design, fashion design, pixel art, and sketching.

"I am a digital artist who enjoys designing characters for fantasy and video games. I also to posters and book covers, creature concept art book illustrations, and character commissions."

— CAEL JOHNSON

FOR MORE VISIT:

Galification Media is committed to bringing high quality stories, in various genres and settings, to life through all forms of media from print to digital mediums as well as cinematic media.

Check out our other works at:

www.GalificationMedia.com